DON'T
CALL ME A
HURRICANE

Also by Ellen Hagan

Watch Us Rise (with Renée Watson)
Reckless, Glorious, Girl

DON'T CALL ME A

HURRICANE

ELLEN HAGAN

BLOOMSBURY

NEW YORK LONDON OXFORD NEW DELHI SYDNEY

BLOOMSBURY YA
Bloomsbury Publishing Inc., part of Bloomsbury Publishing Plc
1385 Broadway, New York, NY 10018

BLOOMSBURY and the Diana logo are trademarks of Bloomsbury Publishing Plc

First published in the United States of America in July 2022
by Bloomsbury YA

Text copyright © 2022 by Ellen Hagan

Bloomsbury books may be purchased for business or promotional use. For information
on bulk purchases please contact Macmillan Corporate and Premium Sales Department
at specialmarkets@macmillan.com

Library of Congress Cataloging-in-Publication Data
available upon request
ISBN 978-1-5476-0916-1 (hardcover) • ISBN 978-1-5476-1016-7 (e-book)

Book design by Jeanette Levy
Typeset by Westchester Publishing Services
Printed and bound in the U.S.A.
2 4 6 8 10 9 7 5 3 1

To find out more about our authors and books visit
www.bloomsbury.com and sign up for our newsletters.

For: Araceli & Miriam & all the ways you love & honor the earth
& all the ways you tell your own stories.

For my brilliant & thoughtful students,
especially the young IPEP poets
at Marble Hill High School for International Studies.
I stand in awe of the way you speak up
& make certain your voices are heard.

For the young climate activists who use their voices
& their art to create change.

Here is to a lifetime of rising up alongside of you all.

DON'T CALL ME A
HURRICANE

The Ocean Calls

"Grab your board," Isa shouts,
throwing open the screen door
letting sunshine and cool breeze
into our living room. "Let's roll!"

"Already halfway there," I say,
smiling while throwing on a T-shirt.

"*Water Is Sacred*," Isa reads. "I love that. Turn around."
On the back: *Rebel Planet*. "Ohhhh, yes! Is that new?"

"New, as in made it from an old shirt of my mom's,
but yup, and I made one for you too."

"Of course you did. This bond . . ."

"Unbreakable," we both say.
I give Isa (short for Isabella) a quick hug and head outside.

"You know I'm coming too, right?" Ada says,
holding her boogie board.

"Me too?" Jack calls, running down the stairs,
nearly crashing into us.

"You know it," Isa answers.
"My brothers and sister are outside.
But if we don't hurry, Holyoke will be packed.
And it's about to be summertime for real.
So you know those first-time surfers
will be trying to take all our good, good waves.
So come on!"

Outside, we ride

All five of us. Me and Ada and Jack.
Isa, Mateo, Rio, and Marisol. Neighbors. Best friends.
Family. Known each other since birth.
Mess with one of us, you mess with all of us.
In our lives forever.

Isa and I take the lead. Standing up on our beach cruisers
calling directions as we take over the boulevard.
Avoid the family-sized, four-person bikes
that all the newbies rent from Seashore Rides.
Avoid the runners with their fancy sneakers
who are new in town
and the bikers who think we're in their way.
In the summer months this place is full of people
who think we are the ones
who don't belong.

We pay them no mind. Take our time.
Know every part of this island.
Know the tides and salt in the air.
Know how to stay steady
when it sometimes
feels like
we're
sinking.

But we stay above

We're the oldest at seventeen, so we keep it steady.
Balancing boogie boards and surfboards.
Taking up all the space.
Spreading out, peddling and pushing,
riding and laughing. This is our home.
No matter what the people visiting
think of us and the way we roll through.
Ada and Mateo cover the back.
They're fifteen and think they're older than us.
We all know the truth but let them pretend.
Jack and Rio ride the middle.
They're eleven and couldn't care less
where they fit in.
Marisol stays close.
The baby of our crew.
She's ten and none of us
take our eyes far away from her.
Truth is, it doesn't much matter
where we fall in line.
We've all got one goal.
Getting to the ocean,
where we feel
most
alive.

Steady & Wild

Once beneath the waves, my whole body
becomes a type of magic, a kind of calm
that settles over me and I can just be.
The water relaxes me
and riles me up at the same time.

She breaks & winds. Loops & bumps
below the surface. All tremble & glow.
She is comforter & healer. All salt & float.
Out on the waves, I'm free.

Free.

   Free.

Beach Daze

We spend the whole day like this. All seven of us
bonded by waves that rise and fall. Sunshine and sand.

Beneath each turn we are weightless. Wild and loose.
Jumping from low tide to high, breaking through

the surface to glide. Every day of summertime
will be like this. Like us. Sitting lifted on top

of the dunes. Jetting from hot sand to salt water
the sea cooling us down. Doing it over again and again.

Every day possible, we will spend
lazing by the shore. Telling jokes and stories

our voices looping together and riding us through.
Boogie boards in the morning, skimboards at noon,

bodysurfing until sundown. We've always known
all the beaches and backroads that lead us here.

This has always been our home and we've spent
every moment loving it as much and as hard as we can.

"Ice Cream Truck!"

Marisol shouts as soon as she hears the song.
All of a sudden, she is running high speed
all the way up the dunes.
Jack and Rio rush behind.
Grab our beach bag and let her lead the way.

Ice cream is part of our summer every day, too.
Cherry Italian ice, chocolate cones with sprinkles,
strawberry shortcakes, sno-cones, ice-cream sandwiches,
and vanilla with a chocolate shell. Popsicles and push pops.
Everything sweet. This is the way to love summertime.

"I like it most out here," Jack says, burying his toes
deep inside the cool sand of the dunes, leaning back.
His face to the sun.

"Me too," Rio agrees.

"Same," Ada adds.

All of them with their faces soaking
in the sun. Starfished bodies spread out.

But I always like it best beneath the waves,
salt water surrounding me,
silence below water
drifting and floating away
not sitting on the shoreline,
but in the middle of it all.

We ride wave after wave

Isa and I have been boogie boarding and bodysurfing
and surfing since we were born. *Water babies*, they called us.

Swimming from the time we arrived. Both of us at ease
in the ocean. Learned it from our moms, who grew up
on this same small island. Knowing each other. Sisters.

Yara and Nina—they grew up on Essex Street. In and out
of each other's houses. Grew up loving salt water and sand.
Grew up cooking, eating, laughing, and loving the tides.

Yara bringing her roots from Puerto Rico
and my mom bringing hers from Italy.
Their cultures laying the groundwork,
flavors intertwined so their kitchens create fireworks.
Those skills and that power and all that electricity
turning into Crabs 'n' Cakes, their seafood shack
that served the whole island before the storm
and has been slowly starting to build back after it.

The two of them are our models and guides.
That's how we came to be.
Raised together. Crew. Squad. Crowd. Team.
Troop. Band. Company. Herd.
Not family by blood,
but family by history. Family by memory.
And what we hold on to.
And what we carry with us.
And what we owe the ocean
And all that it has carried for us.

Been learning how to honor
and respect this haven.
This shelter.
Our sanctuary from the start.

The Jersey Shore according to MTV

is different than the way we see ourselves.

"This is our home,"
my mom and Yara are always saying,
"And no matter what anyone says
about where we live, it's ours to love.
Don't let anyone put it down
or make you feel less than
because of where you come from.
Own it. Love it. Celebrate it."

My dad says, "This place is misunderstood.
People are always trying to figure us out,
always trying to tell us who we are.
We tell our own stories. Don't need a crew
to document our drama. We tell it
the way we see it. Tell our own truth."

According to MTV, the Jersey Shore is loud,
wild, and always full of curse words and rowdy ways,
sun rays and no sunscreen. Fake tans and stories.
A boardwalk soap opera. All tragedy, all the time.

But they're wrong. One hundred percent
that is not who we are.

The Jersey Shore, according to us

Is everything we love. It is sunshine and sea. All salt water
and seashells. The shoreline and sunsets sinking into the bay
and rising over the ocean. It is surfboards floating
on Holyoke Avenue & kids learning to skimboard
in the shallow water. Riding waves from the time
the lifeguards arrive until they pack it up each night.
and afterward, building sandcastles that topple and fade.
Digging holes enough to bury ourselves up to our necks
and then breaking free. The ice cream trucks that rip down
Center Avenue and the Ferris wheel that reaches up
to the sky at Fantasy Island. The bumper cars
and Dragon roller coaster we ride dozens of times
on Pay One Price Friday nights. Shopping at Farias,
pizza slices from Bay Village, and Swedish fish
from the Ship's Wheel in Harvey Cedars. It's cheesesteaks
with Bar-B-Whew and wing night at the Chicken or the Egg,
but no one calls it that, so it's wing night at the Chegg
and everyone is there. The kids you grew up with,
the ones you love, one you can't stand. Because home
is some of the time complicated. It's paddleboarding
and afternoon kayaking off the end of the island in Holgate.
It's surfing, skateboarding, walking, running, and riding bikes
with no shoes on. Your feet getting tough and rugged
enough to get through anything. Feeling free and loose.
It's drifting and floating and almost sinking, but someone
pulling you up just in time. This is the place we all grew up
and grew into who we are. It's locals and tourists.
It's born here and just visiting. And for those of us
who were born right here in Long Beach Island, New Jersey,
this place is our own. We call it—home.

Anyone who lives on an island

knows that once you get on it
it's sometimes hard to get off.
And the same goes once you're off
to get back on. Distant and close.

Long Beach Island is connected
by a long, far-reaching road we all
call the Causeway, also known
as the Manahawkin Bay Bridge.

The steel structure that spans
across the bay, carrying cars
from Route 72—from Stafford
Township—from the mainland.

Bikes and bodies can travel too,
but mostly it's cars and trucks.
Leaving that landlocked life
and showing up to water everywhere.

From the top of the bridge, you can see
out to Little Egg Harbor and Barnegat
Bay and all the way to Atlantic City,
almost hear the slot machines ringing.

Smell the salt in the air. Something
about that road across from land
to sea, changes a person. Shaped us.
For sure, made us who we are.

Standing at the edge of the world

That's what it feels like standing on the shoreline
and looking out at our lives on this island.

water is water is water is water is water is water
is water is water is water is water is water is water

So this is the only place we know. The one we return to.
The one that stays rooted and lodged in our hearts.

Imprinted and memorized in our bones. This is shelter
and the storm. All at the same time. We cruise slow home.

Isa, me, Ada, Mateo, Jack, Rio, and Marisol. All seven.
A line of bodies worn out from water and wind.

The ride is slow. A kind of surrender. We say good night
and I remember to be thankful for summer and Saturdays.

All the weekends we'll spend in a kind of haze. Timeless.
Holding our breath underwater and coming up for air.

Back at Home

We throw our gear in the shed
and take turns in the outside shower.
Each of us competing for who can go faster.
Waste less water. Ada always wins.

"That's because you don't actually wash anything,"
Jack says, jumping in after.
"How do I always lose?" he asks.

I sit on the sidewalk outside of our house.
The place we all grew up in
could have been called a shack before the hurricane.
It was small but just ours. A perfect beach bungalow
that everyone crammed into. It was tiny but fit us just fine.
There was one large bedroom in the way back
where the kids all slept and one bedroom in the front
where my folks set up. A living room big enough
for two bulky couches and loads of bookshelves.
And a kitchen where we could all crowd around the table,
bumping and elbowing.

None of that mattered.
Our whole street was full of the same families.
Year-rounders who spent most of our time out of doors.
Home in the sea, home outside.

After the hurricane

The house felt abandoned.
Everything washed away.
Lost in the waves.
All of our books and treasures.
My old journals and seashells. Gone.
Photographs and albums, cards and memories.
All that we held so close. Let go and left behind.
The whole block said goodbye to their shared history.
Waved it away.

After the hurricane, the whole street changed.

One house after the other.
Slow at first, but now—years later,
we are one of the only ones to stay put.

Our house looks like a storm itself.
All rambling with additions and extra around the edges.
New floors, but not fancy wood ones.
We built up like they told us to, like they forced us to.
If we didn't raise our house,
the ocean or the price of inflated insurance
would take us down for sure.
So we lifted it up and away from the ground
and the greedy, greedy sea.
And the greedy, greedy insurance agencies.
Now we kids sleep huddled in the attic,
which has an exit to the roof,
the only place I feel like I can be by myself.

Away from the ramble. The chaos.
Now home feels unpredictable.
With million-dollar beach and bay-front properties
popping up all around us.
Seeming to make fun of where we live
just by being built up beside us.
They mock us.
Rising up,
they look down on us from above.

Back then

Life felt sweet and free.
Like everything was full of laughter,
sugar, waves, luck, and love.
Like we could spend all our time
jumping waves, loving the sunshine.
Loving each other
knowing nothing could hurt us
or take it away.

Knowing home was a constant.
Knowing home was a lighthouse.
Knowing home would always be there
and even if we didn't have much
we had each other.
And enough for a treat
to get us through the summer.
And enough of the ocean
that was free for us to love.

Knowing nothing could take that away.

Ever.

Until it did.

When we were kids

The flooding on the island
was fun and exciting.

We didn't know enough
to be worried about it.

Didn't think splashing around
in the streets could lead to so much damage
and destruction. Felt like when I was a kid,
there was so much I didn't know,
so much I was curious about,
but now it feels like there's too much.

Too much information
rattling around in my brain.
Can't get any of it out,
so it keeps me awake at night.

Sea level rise. Watching the way
the earth is heating up.
All the time.
Loving something
that could take away
everything
and everyone
I love.

All it would take

was one powerful storm
to tear us all apart.
Just one tropical cyclone
to rip everything to shreds.
Upturn houses
and lives and families.
Only one rapidly rotating system
to uproot us all.
A hurricane for the record books.
One that would look at our house
and our island. And laugh
while wreaking havoc on everything
in its path.

This is what people were always
warning us about.
Meteorologists and newscasters
and old neighbors and family members
making homes on solid ground
all reminding us:

You live on a barrier island.
Your life is on the fault line.
A risk just by living.
You absorb energy
and protect the coastline.
But when in danger
who will protect you?
Who will save you?
And what will be left
if they do?

My Whole Family

Just waiting.
Not paying
attention.
Or not wanting
to believe it.
See it.
Own it.

My friends and me
looking
away.

Until
we were
face to face
with a hurricane.

My father used to call me a hurricane

wild & unruly
rowdy & messy
fast & reckless

unmoving & impulsive
headstrong & willful
unexpected & quick
electric & fleeting
floating & flying
scrappy & breakneck

all the time
    moving
& flowing
& hurried
& flashing

& free

    free

       free

Now—

we are careful
not to compare anything
to a hurricane
because we know
how dangerous
& destructive it can be.
We know its toll.
From the US
to the Caribbean
to China
to Canada
to Cuba
& on & on.
Wrecking lives
& families across the globe.
We know its winds & rains.
Floods & rising waters.
We know the damage.
& the loss.
We know the trauma
& the pain
& the doubled over
& the weeping
& my mother holding on to us
to save us
from the storm.
How the shape
of our lives
changed
forever.

We know
the cost.

Now, all the water that surrounds me

feels like it's a risk. Tides overflowing.
King tides and fear of the ocean meeting the bay.
Riptides pulling me in.

When I can't sleep, I make a list of all the oceans
and bodies of water that stay on my mind.
The ones that circle and float inside my head.
Sink me if I'm not careful.

Mid-Atlantic Ridge, West Indies, Canary Islands,
Rio Grande Rise, Pacific and Atlantic Oceans,
Southern and Indian Oceans, Red and Arabian Seas

Study the massive map that takes over our bedroom.
Study each rise and how water can become flood
and drench. Drown and submerge.

Seychelles, Philippine and Tasman Seas, Java
and Mediterranean Seas, Gulf of Aden,
Somali Basin, Galapagos and Cape Verde Islands

Say the names out loud. Over and again.
Imagine sailing the world to study what it means
to stay alive when the planet is plunging below.

Central Pacific Basin, Gulf of Alaska, Labrador
and Norwegian Seas, Arctic Ocean, South China
and Black Seas, Gulf of Guinea, Caribbean Sea

Consider how small we really are—each of us struggling
to stay afloat. I go on and take a big gulp of air.
Hold my breath and prepare for what's next.

How is it possible to love something so much

but still be terrified of it? Hold it close
but worry it could sink you?
Want to live beside it
but scared it could
end you?

These questions
stay lodged inside me
carry them with me all
along the way. My therapist
is always asking me to analyze
my relationship to water, to the ocean.

Always asking
how it shapes me
changes me
pushes
and pulls me
brings me
back
to myself.

And every time
I think about
my people:
my family
and friends
and how all of us
are linked to water
to swimming
to treading

to hoping
to breathing
to staying above
to surviving.

Family Time

We sit around hungry, waiting for extra food
that Mom always brings home from the shack.
We look like straight up mixes of each other.
My dad, hairy and tall; my mom, petite and small.
Each of us is a split version of them.

From my dad, I got dark, thick, wavy hair.
And from my mom, I got height and size.
We share all the same clothes,
doubling our closet size, which is good
since we never buy anything new anyhow.
Jack is the same kind of small.
Ada says she got her strength from our dad,
his height and thickness too.
She brags and leaves us in the dust
when we race in the bay.

My hair is finally growing out
from the last time I chopped it all off.
Not afraid to change what I look like
or how I show up anymore.
Down past my chin now,
I wear it loose and wild.
Five earrings up my right ear
and three up my left.
Been begging for a nose ring
and a tattoo of a wave across the inside
of my wrist, but mom says wait until I'm 18.

Me and my brother and sister with tanned skin
from the sunshine and our Sicilian ancestors.

My body strong enough from surfing and swimming
and too much on my mind
to care about what makeup to wear
or what clothes to buy
or what's in style.
I'm just me.

From my dad
I got a loud and rowdy voice
and all the ways we show up wild in the world.
Unruly and rebellious.
From my mom I got skills in the kitchen,
and learned how to sauté the freshest shrimp
and make baked ziti that'll make you cry.
Got her willingness to risk everything.

Risk-taker

from both of them.
Double, double.
Their work ethic
and nonstop,
their push and energy.
We all got their drive,
their passion for the ocean
and island life.
Their love of kayaking
and paddleboarding,
collecting seashells
and memories.
All of this life
straight from them.

Try this

my mom says, opening up cartons
of leftovers from the restaurant
where Mom and Yara live 'round the clock
from Memorial Day to Labor Day.
Labor of deep love, they say.

She feeds my dad a forkful of crab cake
doused in hot sauce and tartar. Tears
come to his eyes and we all gather around.
Open up seasoned fries, fried oysters,
onion rings, blackened and grilled scallops
dredged straight from the floor of the Atlantic Ocean.
Creamy seafood bisque. Everything sustainable.
Everything made by my mom's and Yara's hands.

Year-round and local is what my mom and dad live by
and the way they've taught us to be in the world.

"You know I love the tourists"

Mom starts in. We all give her a look like *yeah, right.*

"I do! Well, I appreciate them. They make the island work.
And I will not lump them all together.
And you shouldn't either." She looks right at me
knowing my own issues with the part-timers.

"But . . . there are a few who treat us like we're only here
to take care of them. Like we don't live and love here.
It feels like they think this place is a playground
to just drop in on. Just land to build and build on.
With no thought or concern about the tides
or how to protect against erosion or the dunes.
It's just part-time living for them, so they don't see
everything we work so hard for. And I don't think
they love this place enough to just leave it alone."
She pauses and my dad walks over,
starts to rub her shoulders.

"I want to find a way to live with them,
and not always feel like we're fighting against them.
I just don't even know if it's possible."

We stay quiet. No one says a word or has a solution.

"Come on. Enjoy. We've still gotta eat, don't we?"

We talk endless and over each other

so that the whole meal is like a concert.

"Pass the ketchup. Anyone need sriracha?"

"Wild riptides that came right over my head."

"Bit it out there on the waves!"

"Construction is out of control. Worked to the bone."

"How long was the line at Crabs 'n' Cakes?"

"You mean to tell me they are building more houses?"

"Hope you all kept an eye on Marisol. She's the baby."

"They say this is gonna be the busiest summer ever."

"Just gotta make all the money we can
before hurricane season comes around again."

"You know you can never be too safe."

"This is what survival on this island looks like now."

"Protect what you can, but always know
you could lose it all in an instant."

Before the hurricane

We never talked about survival in this same way.
Never imagined our lives uprooted and taken over by loss.

But now we stay close, threaded together holding
what's left. All the time staying thankful.

Food like prayer in our house. Finding solutions
and struggling together to preserve what we love.

My mom and Yara feeding everyone they know.
Both neighbors and strangers. Welcoming them.

My dad pushing for sustainable building.
Maintaining the integrity of the sand beneath our feet.

Me and my siblings and our crew of friends working
to educate ourselves and the tourists who arrive.

This island is the only home we've ever known.
And everything we do now. Every act we make

every single action we take. Is working
to make this place stay afloat. Stay ours. Forever.

Lifeguard on Duty

I show up to the beach at nine a.m. ready to swim.
The bay is quiet and calm, so I swim alone.
Lap after lap to get my mind ready for the day.
Freestyle out and back. Let my body float along.
Nine thirty a.m. and Isa shows up. We are a team out here.
The two of us trained together, took the test together
and now we keep the people and the bay safe together.

"You know you're not supposed to be swimming alone,"
she says as I'm drying off. We move the lifeguard stand
down toward the shoreline and start to get set up.

"It was just a few laps and besides I couldn't wait for you,
since I know you needed your beauty sleep," I tease.
Isa is always up way past midnight
and I am awake first thing in the morning.
The way we see it, one of us is alert
at all hours of the day,
watching, waiting,
paying close attention.

"You're here now," I say, pulling her in for a hug.

Steady

As soon as the lifeguard stand is set up,
we both climb to the top.
Nine forty-five a.m. and all is quiet.
So we both go silent too. Feet planted,
shoulders rolled back. Breath steady.
Close our eyes. Pay attention to our heart rates.
And go under. Every morning we meditate.
It started as a joke since my therapist suggested
it would help bring me down when anxiety
started to seep into my head. We'd laugh
and say we needed to slow down and focus.
And then the joke started to be serious
when my panic attacks felt closer
and more real and scarier and my breath
became lost to me.

"Keep trying," my therapist would say.
"You have to learn how to be strong
and steady in the world. Even if everything
is swirling all around you. Scared is okay.
But you cannot let it define you.
Deep breath. In and out.
Count all the things you are thankful for
and the meditation will become a habit."

She was right.

What I Am Thankful For

waves
wind
winding roads
sand in my hair
breath
breathing
weightless
home
seashores
ocean floors
shrimp
scallops
my mom's voice
her arms holding me
my dad's stories
his laugh—high and loud
Ada
Jack
Isa
Mateo
Rio
Marisol
surfing
riding
swimming
diving
feeling
crying
meditating
cooking

writing
this moment
right now
always

Surf City Bay Beach

They put me and Isa on the bay beach in Surf City
and we both love it. The calm waves hitting shore.
The families with kids who run and splash
each time like it's the first. Sometimes it is.
They scream and shout to each other and us.
I love the way the days unfold beneath the sunshine.
The way you can spend every hour devoted to nature.
To the land and sea. And I am thankful for the people
who make their summers here. Even the tourists
who fill our sandy beaches and stores,
who spend their money at Crabs 'n' Cakes
and post about our island all over social media,
saying how much they love it and how wonderful
all the people who live here are.
I know they sometimes talk about us as if
we are part of the attraction, but on a day like this
when the bay is packed with laughter and joy
I can't help but feel we are all a part of this place
and we should do everything in our power
to make this island last. To keep it afloat.

"This Is Our Summer"

Isa reminds me. "The last one before senior year.
This is the summer we've been dreaming of."

"Really?" I ask. We are leaning back on the lifeguard stand.
Off duty now and watching the sun set over the bay.
"It kind of feels like last summer,
except for now we have jobs. What else has changed?"

"Oh my god! You are such a downer. Come on.
Be positive. Isn't that what your therapist says? Right?"

I nod, knowing Isa is the only one who knows
the insides of my mind. The only one
I've told about therapy. About my anxiety.
About how much I've been holding on to and for how long.

"No, I know. You're right, you're right.
I am supposed to think of everything that I am thankful for.
You, of course," I say, pulling her into a side hug.
Resting my head on her shoulder. "This," I point to the bay.
To the orange and deep yellow of the sunset.
"I am sooo thankful we got jobs. Yes to that!
And to the work," I say.
"The work of helping shape this island."

"Our home," Isa says. "Not giving up. Or in.
Not letting this island get run over by everyone else.
Construction and developers who think
they are doing something for *us*," she says.
"When really, they're only doing it for this," she adds,
rubbing her thumb against her fingers,

meaning money. Meaning excess.

Meaning more, more, more.

Meaning less for us.

Less for those who have put in the work.

Less for the families left behind after the hurricane.

After the destruction.

Those of us leftover.

Those of us who stayed.

How It All Started

Maybe it was when the local news
said we were struggling.
Called our island forgotten
and left over. Kept asking: *who will stay
after all this?* Said we were lost
and didn't know how we would go on.
Said our home was uninhabitable.

Maybe it was all the articles
about king tides and rising seas.
And how we needed to protect
what we love. About the risk
of living on a barrier island.
The risk of global warming,
how we were at the center
and needed to leave.

Maybe it was the insurance agencies
who said we didn't have the right claims
or the correct insurance. Was it flood
or wind damage? Or what exactly
can be insured? In a storm?

Maybe it was all the local banks
who wanted to grant loans to anyone
who lived outside of the island.
Didn't trust us or our history
or experience or our connection
to home.

Maybe it was relatives who told us
to move far, far away. Said Philly
or Barnegat or Manahawkin
would be a better fit.

Everyone all the time saying
they didn't trust or believe
we had it in us.

Maybe our teachers.
Who didn't even live
on the island.
And said it was better
to start all over again.

But something switched

something ticked
inside of us.
Told us to read more
about the planet
& our island
& share more
& most of all
stand up for what matters
& what we believe in
& make it right
somehow.
Some way.
Together.

Clam Cove Reserve

This is the place that stays on our minds.
24 acres of coastal marshland that sits
just outside our doors.
Basically it is our backyard.
The place we have spent every day of our lives.
It was always considered sacred,
our safe space.
The land preserved
for so many animals and species,
songbirds, ospreys, egrets,
herons, and gulls, ducks,
mussels, and blue crabs
and especially
the northern diamondback terrapins.
Nesting habitats for the native turtles to this coast.
And more than that, it is a space to protect
and secure, safeguard against the elements.
When the storm wrecked everything,
it pushed sand from the ocean beaches here
and everything changed.
The developers looked at this spot
as theirs. Saw it ruined and trashed
and so they saw buildable lots
with multimillion-dollar price tags
and families buying up land
that would change the shape of everything.
And put the island at risk of overdevelopment
and put the natural habitats at risk of destruction
and put the turtles at risk of extinction
and our whole way of life at risk of disappearing.

It Can't Be All About the Money

But lately it seems that way.
Because the push to develop the marshlands
is going strong. And there is construction all around us.
Not just Clam Cove Reserve is at risk,
but every street surrounding Holgate
is erupting with new construction.
Bulldozers and teams of workers 'round the clock.
Tearing down old houses and rebuilding
as if nothing was there before.
Every street getting a facelift. A new look.
Demolishing old homes to build bigger
and more elaborate mansions.
Massive structures built on stilts
rise up all around us.
Overwhelming storm drains and waterways
and pushing us all to the edge.
To the brink.
Everywhere we look, the same name
on all of the new houses
Hope/Hart Construction.
Even the name
feels like a joke
some cruel trick
they are playing on us.
Because none of it
feels like it has anything
to do with hope.

This summer, we're fighting back

Against the story that we're victims
that we're lost because of the storm.
That we can't survive without money
coming in from the outside.
That we're not enough on our own.
That we won't make it
without fancy new hotels and restaurants,
clothes and souvenir shops
and condominiums with hot tubs
and cabanas that offer privacy
and luxury and seclusion.

So we all get together.
All of the local lifeguards
along with a bunch of kids we grew up with
and even some of our friends from school
who don't even live on the island
but care enough to show up with us.
In solidarity for climate change.
In solidarity with us.

We've started to meet once a week,
coming together to plan actions
against Hope/Hart Construction
and their vision of changing the landscape.
Pushing back on their plans to develop
the marshlands specifically,
but all the endless development too.
We prep upcoming events,
surf competitions, block parties. Anything
to grab the attention of local news and media.

Finding people to follow our struggle. And it's true
we are still struggling all these years later.
Still watching the rising tides, still

re-building
re-zoning
re-doing
re-imagining

still wondering how we'll become whole
again. After losing so much. We push on.

Call ourselves the LBI Climate Justice Seekers

Everyone is welcome.
No one turned away.
This is group work.
We are in it.
Together.

Collective leadership.
That's what we've been learning about.
There is not just one leader at the top.
We all show up together.
Learning and teaching at the same time.
Not just one voice, but many.
How do we all claim space?
Show up our full selves.
At the ready. As one.

Friday, July 1 | Climate Justice Seekers Meet-Up
Nine weeks to demolition . . .

On Fridays, we come together
in solidarity with Fridays for Future,
meeting first as a big group at the local school
and then breaking into our smaller working teams.

Today our team sets up at Bay Village.
We are inspired by this call for action
around the globe. We show up,
we rise up. We educate. We learn.
Our table is outside of Yara and Nina's shack
while they serve seafood dinners to tourists.
We want them to know what we're about.
It is packed.

We set up a table with flyers and pamphlets
created in our team.
It's Isa, me, Zach, and Mia,
our best friends from school.
Every small group has a focus.
Saving Clam Cove Reserve is ours.
Each of us shows up after work.
Mia runs the slides at the water park,
Zach runs double duty
and scoops endless ice-cream cones
at Scoop's Up in Schooner's Wharf
and serves the best coffee
on the entire island at Brew You.
Their barista skills are magic,
so today, they come loaded up
with cups of broken-up waffle cones

and layers of cotton candy and strawberry
and lattes all around. We call this good luck
since we know everyone who works
in this rambling ship and wharf
that holds stores and restaurants,
places to buy souvenirs and sunglasses,
pizza shops and blown glass, pottery
and Swedish fish. It's the place everyone
comes together. Whether you grew up here
or whether you're just visiting for the day.

"This is the way I like to protest," Zach says,
handing us each a coffee. Zach is nonbinary
and uses they/them pronouns.
Their hair is dyed hot pink down the middle
and shaved on each side
and Zach is so tall and skinny that everything
they wear hangs loose on their body.
Mia's pixie cut is making me think
of chopping off my hair again
and she always has the perfect clothes
that fit her thick curves. She stays confident.
Isa sits beside us, scooping up her ice cream.
She's as tall as Zach with curly black hair
and the two of them beside each other
look like they'd be perfect surfer kid spokespeople
for our SAVE THE CLAM COVE RESERVE T-shirts.

We talk to everyone who comes up
and even call out to people shopping around.
They should know that our small island
is at risk. All the time.
They call it: Water risk

That's what we're experiencing
and have been since the hurricane
and since every storm that has
rocked this place ever since.

We can add erosion
and risk of overdevelopment too.
Disappearing beaches and sand dunes.

Knowing construction can change
the whole shape of this place,
could put us all at risk too.

Water Risk

Risk of flooding.
Risk of damage
Risk of infrastructure decay.
Risk of decay itself.
Risk to homes.
Risk to shelter.
Risk to lives.
Risk to physical health.
Risk to mental health.
Risk to emotional health.
Risk to stability.
Risk to the everyday.
Risk to waterways.
Risk to causeways.
Risk to the bay.
Risk to the ocean.
Risk to our futures.
Risk to it all.

The hurricane is my leader—

pushing me to wake up every day

exhausting
roiling
rocking
biting back

the waves keep coming
the shore keeps disappearing
lined with motels, marinas
and second homes,
the Army Corps of Engineers
keeps replenishing
rearranging the beaches
the dunes keep sliding
out of view.
It is all a temporary solution
Short term and losing time.

Waves reaching out
receding
pealing awake
putting me to shame
pushing me to act
keeping me awake
each night.

And all this work now
is to save Clam Cove Reserve

save the marshlands
from being developed and built up.
Crushing what little land is left.
As greedy as possible.

We are here—set up in Bay Village

spending the whole afternoon
talking to locals and tourists
and those who don't know us
or what we represent.
Making sure they know
we oppose construction
of the Hope/Hart project
which promises
multimillion-dollar homes
with lots of land
and the most beautiful bay views
by demolishing and ripping up
Clam Cove Reserve,
ruining natural habitats
and making the island
feel like a playground for the rich.

They are already building everywhere else.
Why can't they just leave our cove alone?

But these developers are relentless.
Showing up here right after the hurricane
and knocking down old houses
to build their monster homes,
wrecking our way of life
and building for everyone new.
And they are not stopping there
so even our one safe place
will be torn apart if we don't stop them.
And we're up against a deadline
that gets closer every day of summer.

September 1, to be exact

Demolition day.
Day of reckoning
and wreckage.

First day of construction
just day one of destruction.
Bulldozers moving in
to crush habitats,
ruin whole ecosystems
endanger even more species
for rooftop decks
and views from the ocean to the bay.

Hope/Hart Construction
and their project to uproot the marshlands
is coming to destroy our backyard
for profit in their own pockets.

But not if we have anything
to do with it. We are strong
and will show up no matter what.

Besides it is only the first week of July,
so we have all the summertime we need.
And all I know is we're destined to stop it.

"Party . . . tonight!"

Isa says, leaning in
and snapping me out of my imagination.

"I'm too tired," I say, begging off. I can feel my bed
calling to me. "I'm out. But maybe next week?"

"No, no, no. You said this was the summer you'd be free,"
Isa reminds me.

"You said this was the summer you were gonna be wild,"
Zach says, grabbing a French fry from my plate.

"You said this was the summer you were gonna get loose
and make out with whoever you wanted to,"
Mia adds, laughing with them now.

"I did not say all of that! Especially not the making out part.
There's no way I . . ." They stare at me. "Okay, maybe I said it,
but it was the stress from school talking. I'm good now.
I don't need to be kissing anyone to make this summer
one to remember."

They stay staring at me.

"We're just saying," Zach says. "It's been a whole week
of summer. And we only really have nine weeks left.
You know I've been keeping track of that. Nine weeks
until senior year and we . . . especially you, haven't done
anything except work and volunteer for the island.
You can't let the whole summer go to waste and not
do something for you."

Zach has a way of making things a bit more dramatic
than they really are, but in some ways they're right.
A summer without a little fun isn't really a summer
at all.

"You gotta be there," Mia adds,
all of them teaming up now.

"Fine. You're right, you're right. I can't let summer
go to waste. I'll go."

Prep Time

We get ready at my house. With so many kids
and so little space, adding more people is no big deal.

Ada and Jack sit on the floor and rate our outfits.
We go in and out of the bathroom, changing
and rearranging what we're planning to wear.

Zach and Isa have the best closets on the island.
Every weekend we thrift for secondhand
in Barnegat Light and on the mainland,
which is where they find all kinds
of good things. Old leather jackets,
jeans that look like they've been perfectly worn in,
and old T-shirts from all over the Jersey Shore.
Tonight I'm in a shirt that Zach cut the sleeves off of
and fringed the bottom. It says *Surf & Dive* on the front
and *Hudson House* on the back.

Used to be we'd beg our folks to take us
to the mall, but once we started getting caught up
in climate justice groups, we changed our ways,
figured fast fashion and buying new
weren't worth landfills filling up every time
we grew out of something.

Zach always says they're ahead of their time
and has been thrifting since they were a kid,
and I guess that's kind of true for all of us.
Hand-me-downs have been a way of life.
All four of us with working-class families,
with just enough—never too much.

"Makeup?" Zach and Mia ask, holding up
my very small bag that carries what little I wear.
Lip gloss and mascara is about as far as I go,
but Zach loves to add a little extra.
To both themselves and the rest of us.
So eyeliner is applied all around.

"My blush is from the sun," I say,
pushing them away and posing in the mirror.

"Me too," Zach adds, "and from our Caribbean glow,"
they say, putting their arm around Isa,
sharing their connection—Isa's family from Puerto Rico,
and Zach's mom, who is Panamanian.
Zach's dad is Italian and grew up on LBI,
which brought them back here.

"Could I get some of that?" Mia asks
as she pulls the blush toward her. "The Irish in me
is very pale. I could use some help."

"Can I please come?" Ada asks, stepping in front of Zach,
who is applying blush to Mia's cheekbones.

"Soon," Zach whispers in her ear. "But not yet."

"Your days of partying on Rosemma are coming.
But you know Mom and Dad
want you home with Jack tonight."

"I'm eleven," Jack yells to no one in particular.
"I can watch myself."

"They're gonna be out late," I say, giving them both
a quick hug. "And you know what they say.
Two is always better than one.
I'll be home soon."

"But you know, not too soon," Isa says, air-kissing
everyone, all of us stumbling down the stairs
and out into the warm night.

On Our Way

I can feel the salt air on my face.
Heat leftover from a day spent soaking
in the sun, watching waves & floating,
the ocean still on my skin.
Every star lighting up the sky
& no lights to interrupt the night.

I look out over the marshlands
& can't image big homes
& a shopping center
& floodlights
& more cars & SUVs
driving in & out.

This way of life will be lost on them.
If you're willing to wreck all that is good
just for half a dozen lots,
then you have no idea
what this island means
or know any of the people
who call it their own.

We want this island to stay
quiet
calm
peaceful
full of stars
we can see

& the ones
that guide
us home
each
night.

Party

There's a bonfire on the beach at Rosemma Avenue
and when we get there, it's already packed.
Most of the kids we know,
but there's a crowd that shows up
and you can tell right away
they're only here for the summer.
All of them wearing their shoes
right up to the shoreline.

"Shoobies," Isa whispers at me,
using the word all our folks say
when talking about the tourists.
Somehow coming from old times
when people'd show up at the beach
with shoeboxes full of lunch,
spending time down the shore
but no money in the shops.

Of course, that's definitely not true for these kids,
who all look like they have plenty of money
to spend—wherever they want.
Especially on all these designer sneakers
they're wearing right up to the water's edge.
Shoobies for sure. These new people
are bringing a whole different definition.

The music starts up, we all shout
when we hear our favorite songs
and somehow everyone starts dancing.
Not one care in the world.

Time to let loose.

"Oh, hold up"

Zach says, midway through a dance move.
"I think I know that guy and his friends.
Lemme introduce you."

"No . . . don't worry.
I don't need to meet anybody new tonight,"
I say, swaying with Isa and Mia.

"Speak for yourself," Isa says.
"I can always meet someone new."
She looks to where Zach is pointing,
the bonfire lighting up their faces.
"And they're hot, so . . . bring 'em over."

"I'm good to meet them too," Mia adds.
"You know we know everybody on this whole island.
Might as well see some fresh faces."

"Yeah, it's him," Zach says,
looking over at the crowd.
"I met 'em all last week surfing.
They were crap at it, but one of 'em was cool.
We talked about meeting up again.
Just give me a second."

The New Crowd

Zach brings a whole new group over to us.
All of them friendly and chill, but I feel distant
removed. Somehow protective of my crew
and the island as a whole. I feel this every summer
when the whole place gets turned upside down
to make room for everyone else who drops in.

In the winter, there are roughly 13,000 people
who occupy this island.
From Barnegat Light to Holgate.
We stretch from end to end of the seventeen miles
shore to shore.
Like family, we know and love each other.

But in the summer, multiply that by ten,
and you get 130,000 people from north Jersey,
Connecticut, Pennsylvania, and New York.

They come with their carloads of bicycles and surfboards.
They come for summer rentals, bringing the city
with them. Looking for fancy meals and expensive
everything. They want the island, but they want it
to come with all the things they're used to.
Five-dollar cappuccinos and fifteen-dollar cocktails.

They arrive looking for summer memories,
and they get them. Parking their Land Rovers
on the sand. Buying up all that beachfront property,
building and developing everything they touch.
Somehow that stays stuck in my mind, every time.

Introductions

"Eliza Marino, meet Milo Harris," Zach says,
suddenly standing in front of me
with the tallest, hottest guy I have ever seen.

Milo has his wavy hair pulled up in a topknot,
perfect teeth and a smile that goes on forever.
At least I can't find the beginning or end to it.

"He like really had to meet you," Zach whispers,
and I can't tell if they're drunk or high, but their whisper
is much closer to a shout.

"Zach's right, I did," Milo says to my surprise.
"I mean, I had to meet *the* Eliza Marino.
They call you the wave whisperer. Is that right?"

I look dead at Zach, and we both bust up laughing.
"Uh, no one calls me that. Well, maybe Zach
might have called me that . . . when we were five."

"Oh, oh yeah. I knew that was a joke.
Totally knew Zach was kidding," Milo says,
lowering and shaking his head. Clearly embarrassed.

Why? I mouth at Zach, who comes over to me
and really whispers this time.

"He hasn't stopped looking at you. And you know
he's *FINE*. So just talk to him already."

Take Two

"Hey, should we . . . can we start this over?
Because I didn't really think they called you . . .
or, I mean . . ."

Is he nervous? He's nervous.

I smile suddenly. "It's an honest mistake.
You're not from here. You don't know
what we name ourselves or how we
make fun of . . ." I stop just short.

"The people who aren't from around here.
Is that what you mean?"

I stay quiet. Try and make out who exactly it is
I am standing under the moon with
on this warm July night. At the beginning
of my whole life. *Who is he?*

"I'm Milo," he says again, both of us standing
off, away from the crowd.

"Yeah, I heard," I answer, can't tell why
I'm acting this way or what exactly it is
that both irritates and attracts me about him.

"So, do you live around here?
I mean, did you grow up here? In Beach Haven?"

"This isn't Beach Haven."

"Oh, it's not?"

"Nope. It's Holgate. Once you pass Liberty Ave, you're in a whole different place."

"So, this is where you live? Year round?"

"Yup. I grew up here too. All of us did.
Zach, Mia, Isa—that's my people over there."
I point to the three of them, who are all
looking in my direction. *Hi*, I wave.
"And you're from?"

"New York . . . City"

he answers, and I stop myself from saying, *I knew it.*
But of course he is, with his whole look
that probably costs more than my entire closet.
His designer jeans and T-shirt that fit him perfectly
and probably costs a lot of money to look that worn in.

"But I'm here for the summer. The whole summer,"
he adds, acting as if that makes a difference to me.

"Learning to surf?" I ask, smiling up at him again.
Somehow, I can't help myself.

"Yeah, well, that and also working for my dad.
He uh . . . runs a hedge fund, a financial company,
but they do a bunch of other stuff too.
He's got me working with him. Helping out."

"Cool. So, it's just you?"

"You mean do I have any brothers or sisters?" he asks.

I nod, thinking about my big family
and how I'm never alone.

"No, it's just me. Only kid. Well, and my stepmom,
who could technically be my sister, so . . ."

I start to laugh. "Oh no! That can't be good."

"No, it's definitely not good. And she is definitely
the worst. So, I try to avoid both of them

as much as I can. And get out of the house
as much as I can. Which brings me to asking
if you could share your skills and teach me
how to surf?"

I look up at him. *Is he serious?*

"I'm serious," he says. Clearly reading my mind.
"I could use all the help I can get. Also—get me
out of the house, the whole stepmom thing.
Help me out? Please?"

I don't say anything, so he keeps on. "Zach told me
you're number one. The best surfer on the island.
They said you'd teach me everything you know."

"Zach did not say that," I argue.

"Okay, I made up that last part, but they did say
you were the best."

"I don't even know you," I say, taking a step back.

"You could get to know me. You might even like me?"

"I . . . uh . . . yeah. Why don't you give me your number
and I'll call you. If I . . . if I have time. I'll call . . ."
I pull out my phone and type in his name: Milo,
and he types in the numbers to reach him.
Even though I have absolutely no intention
of calling or texting.

"Talk soon?" he says as he walks away.

I nod, knowing we won't
and washing him clear away from my mind.

"Hey—aren't you gonna introduce us?"

I hear a voice while I'm walking away.
"What's your name?"

I turn around and two more people
have walked up and are standing beside Milo.

"And what's your friend's name?"
He points to Isa, who is dancing now.
"I'm Jack. This is Cole."

Milo tilts his head down. Can't tell
if he's embarrassed or nervous.

"I'm Eliza," I say, still standing far off.

"Zach said you're gonna teach our boy
to surf, huh? We're just here for the weekend.
Headed back to the city tomorrow."

"The real world," Cole adds, and they both
start to laugh. Milo does not join in. I notice that.

"No, no. This island is cool. Quiet. Kind of
dead . . . but cool. What'd you say your friend's
name was?" Jack asks, looking at Isa again.

"I didn't," I say. Don't want Isa involved.
Not even sure why I'm still standing here.
"This island . . . isn't trying to be cool.
We don't want to be New York City."

"No fear of that," Cole says.
He laughs to himself.

"Shut up," Milo says. "I'm sorry about them.
Friends from high school. They're drunk,"
he adds, stepping away from them.

"Drunk because there's nothing to do here
except for get drunk. This place sucks,"
Jack adds. "But we did bring beer,"
he says, holding his up and pointing
to the cooler.

"Then good thing you're not staying," I say.
Raise my hand up to say goodbye and walk away.

We leave the party together

Me, Mia, Isa, and Zach.
I go on and take all the beer
that Cole and Jack brought
from the cooler near the fire,
stuff it in my backpack,
and we ride our bikes
away and into the night.
My skin feels warm
the air cool against me
as we cruise and glide
past the Beach Haven Inlet,
the Holgate Marina and Hurley's,
past Lindy's Trailer Park
and Lori's Island End,
finally past the Jolly Roger
where we roll right on
to the end of the island.
Wildlife Refuge.
Nature Conservatory.
Throw our rides
to the side and run
right out to the tide
as it comes in and flows
right out.
This is the beach
that only the locals
know. That's only for us,
the people who've
spent their whole lives
loving this place
as much as we have.
It's ours alone.

The Scoop

Zach looks at me slow. All of us sitting, our toes
tucked into the sand as the water comes in and out.

"If you don't ask him out, then I'm gonna," Zach says.

Isa looks at Zach. "You're serious," she says.

"Yup," Zach replies.

"What about Adam?" Mia asks, who is Zach's
on-again, off-again fling.

"We are open," Zach says. "Besides . . .
it's summertime," they sing. And we all join in
singing about the summer and this night,
out of tune. Laughing and holding on.

Sexuality is fluid, Zach always says. *You love
who you love.* We all agree, but I don't exactly
know what I want or how to feel, especially
since I haven't really dated anyone for real,
and aside from a few hookups,
nobody has really held
my attention
until now.

"I hate to be superficial, and I definitely do not
know what his preferences are, but he's too hot
and summer is too damn short for one of us
to not be hanging out with him. Plus, one of us . . .
and I say it's you . . . Wave Whisperer . . .
has to teach him how to surf. Or at least

how to catch a wave. Because I watched him
and his friends last week. And it was sad.
I was sad for them. He's all city kid out on the waves."

"Uh . . . I don't know about him, but his friends
are the worst. They said this island sucks."

"What?" Isa says. "They suck! Forget them.
But Milo is cute . . . so maybe just put all your focus
on him. And his sexy topknot."

We all laugh. "I don't know," I say. "He gave me
his number and asked me to call or text, so . . .
okay, okay, he's cute. I will admit that.
But nothing else."

They all look at me now. Expecting. Waiting.

"You don't have to marry the guy," Isa says.
"If he wants to hang, just text him. Just see.
Remember what you said about this summer."

"Yes, yes. Fine! Freedom, wild. Summer
of my dreams, blah, blah, blah. I remember."

"So, start acting like it," Zach says.
"Start being the free woman you said you'd be."

The Truth

Zach is right. I know it. Already a week in
and all I have to show for it is five days
on the bay beach making sure kids and families
have a good time and eating endless sno-cones.
Most of the nights home with my family
playing board games or watching movies
and the rest of the time with Isa, Zach, and Mia,
talking endlessly about what we're gonna do
and how we're gonna show up, make a change
and every day I feel like we're closer to losing
the marshlands and losing the love of the island
and I feel it even more standing here, at the end,
looking up at all the new mansions being built
right up onto the shoreline, like they have no
respect for space or nature. Like they don't care
what they wreck or how much space they take up.
I look at the last house being built, the way it rises up.
The name Hope/Hart Construction on a sign in front.
Massive, taking up two lots—still in the wood frame
and all of a sudden my heart starts beating faster
and I can't catch my breath and start to panic.
I know this feeling. Have felt it before.
Have talked to my family and my teachers
and my therapist about this. Panic attacks,
anxiety. Flashbacks . . . and there I am again.
I'm in the eye of the storm and I can't get out.

HURRICANE SEASON

FIVE YEARS AGO

Nonstop

We can't stop watching the Weather Channel.
It stays on like a loop circling us, holding us in.
Huddled on the couch together. Want to move
but can't. Want to pack up, run, hide, disappear.

We can't stop staring and waiting.
Holding our breath.
Holding each other.
Holding on.

According to the weather forecast,
we should be packing our bags
and heading to Manahawkin, the mainland,
for shelter with our aunt and uncle.

According to the governor,
we need to seek shelter fast.

According to the newscaster,
our home will soon be the ocean.

According to my mom, we stay.
According to my dad, we stay.
Ride it out. Just a little longer.
They are scared of losing the new restaurant
and scared of losing our only home
and scared that if we let the storm
scare us away, we will have nothing left
when we return.

We track the storm—

obsess over timeframes
and how long we have
until it's time to panic.
I'm already there,
but try and put on a good face.
Keep my emotions at bay.
The bay, we think,
is rising
and coming for our door.
We watch and wait.
Emotions tied up,
caught,
checked.

Mom paces.
Dad runs up and back
from yard to porch
We wait and watch.

One-one thousand
two-one thousand
three-one thousand

Panic

Jack and Ada stay stuck to me.
Both of them
hanging on everything I say.
Change my face
try and act normal.
Wind howls.
Rain bangs
the windows stay shaking
and my body too.
Trembling beside them.
I am as scared as they are
caught up in our room.
We hear our mom and dad
shouting at each other, at the storm—
to close the windows,
to stay close,
secure the locks
not lose sight.
We stay put.
All of us
huddled close in
next to each other.
Jack cries.
And then Ada sobs,
and it takes all that's inside of me
to keep my eyes dry
when everything around me
is getting soaked.
Drenched.
Underwater.

Alarm

All I hear are sirens.
All I see is wind
and rain. Pelting
and washing
and pouring
outside.

Terrified
we made
the wrong
decision
to stay.

Most of me
hoping
we
make
it
out

alive.

Back on the beach

"Eliza? Hey, Eliza? You okay?" Mia asks,
holding on to my arm. She is always the most gentle
with all of us. Eases us down.
"We lost you for a second," she says.
Always the calm in our storm.
She keeps me steady and focused.

"What? Oh, yeah. I just . . . sorry . . . what'd I miss?
I was just lost in my thoughts, just thinking about everything."

"You've been doing that a lot lately," Isa says,
standing up and brushing sand off her jeans.
"Come on. We gotta get home anyway.
I think you really are as tired as you said you were.
You might need some more sleep."

"Yeah, as if I actually sleep anymore."
They all stop and look at me a little too closely.
"Joking! I'm totally kidding," I say,
trying not to let on that closing my eyes lately
makes me see the past so much more clearly,
and there are so many parts of it
I want to forget.

"No," I say suddenly. "Not yet. We can't go home yet.
You heard Zach. They said it's time to do something
a little bit wild. And I know just the thing."
My bag has the spray paint and Sharpies we'd used earlier,
making flyers and posters at Crabs 'n' Cakes.
"We are about to be remembered.
Come on," I say, draining the last of my beer.

I point at the last house—the one that takes up
the whole beach.
The one that thinks it belongs everywhere.
The one with Hope/Hart Construction
planted on signs around it.
"We're about to make our mark on that
with all of this," I say, opening my bag so they can see
that I'm ready to show them who belongs here.

"Uh, that is not at all what I was thinking . . . ," Zach says,
but gets up at the same time. Always one for adventure
or doing something a little dangerous.

"Yeah, I don't think that's what Zach meant," Isa agrees,
but she's following behind me too.

Crew. Squad. We are in this together.

"No one will know. Besides . . . it's still just a frame.
I just want whoever is behind the whole Hope/Hart
construction team to know that we were here before.
And will be here after . . . too."

We run up the beach

getting caught in the sand, giggling and howling.
The moon is full in the sky.
Race up the dunes, slide down, and sprint up again.

The house looks like a massive skeleton against
all those stars. The Hulk—gigantic and reaching.
We take the stairs two at a time. Landing one.

Bump against each other to the second floor
and again to floor three. The breeze pushing us
up, up. Hundreds of wooden beams hold together
this giant. On the third floor, we stand.
The deck is firm beneath our feet. Can't tell
the rooms apart, but know each one
is bigger than my whole house. Enormous.
Totally consuming. Taking up all the space.

"You think this is a house for like . . . one family?"
Isa asks, careful in the construction. Taking easy
steps from room to room. "It looks like
a freakin' school or community center. I mean . . .
who is gonna even live here? And is it just . . .
for the summer? Like only part-time?
I can't understand it . . ."

We are careful as we roam.
Walls beginning to take shape.
We stare at every turn.
Can't take our eyes away.
Don't feel jealous but feel lost.
Like I can't find the words

or how to mark our existence.
Because we do.
Exist.
And this house makes it seem like
we don't.

Game Plan

Isa figures it out for us. Grabs cans from my bag
and leans back like she's trying to find the right words.
Not our initials or names or anything
that could give us away. Suddenly, she makes waves
in gloss Rolling Surf. I know the color because we obsessed
over the right one. The waves cross from beam to beam. Zach joins in with
gloss Berry, creates waves of their own. And then Mia and I do the same.
Metallic Gold and satin Aqua.
Nothing to let on that it's us.
But showing love for the ocean just the same.
Our ocean. We are protectors of this place. Our home.
We tag as many beams as possible
and tell the whole Hope/Hart team
how we really feel—
We tell them to go home
and that they are not wanted here.
Color and shade them all
to let them know
that they are not welcome.
That the ocean was here
before them.
And will be here
when they're gone.

And just like that. We've done it. Made our mark.

"One last thing," Zach says, looking right at me
and writing "Wave Whisperer" across
one of the biggest beams
for all to see.

"Gotta let 'em know we were here."

I wake up to the smell of onions and peppers

sizzling from downstairs. Dad is cooking
omelettes and fried potatoes. Sliced pineapple
is ready and waiting on the counter.
One of the only meals he loves to make.

I look at my dad, wrapped in Mom's apron,
his shaggy hair a mess and his beard growing
wild. He looks both relaxed and exhausted.

"Okay, okay, finally we have one awake!
I thought it would never happen."
He comes over to kiss my forehead
and as soon as he does, I remember.
Our waves crisscrossing the beams
comes back to me and I realize
that the builders working for the Hope/Hart
construction team are going to arrive on Monday
to see that their work has been damaged.

I realize that they're not the ones
we were trying to hurt, but somehow
they're the ones who will feel it most.

And then I realize that my dad could be the one
to find it. His construction team moves
from house to house on the island. Insulation,
foundation check-ins, walk-arounds.
His crew could go anywhere. He could see
anything. I pour myself a cup of coffee
and push it from my mind. Fill my plate.

"Does no one wake up around here?"
my dad calls up the stairs, just as Ada and Jack
roll down, all groggy and rubbing their eyes.
"It's just us today. Mom's already at the shack,
so who wants to call it? I have the whole day off."

This is my dad's favorite way to spend a day.
Open-ended, flying from one thing to another.
The freedom of a summer Saturday spent
on the seashore.

"Crabbing?" Jack asks. "Let's go out on the boat."

"Perfect," Dad replies, fixing his own plate.
"As long as it holds up."
And that is a big if, since our boat has seen better days.
Fact is, it's a Hail Mary every time we're out on the water.
But we all say our prayers and get dressed. Grab life jackets
and pack lunches. We know the layout, how this works.

Steady.

And we all agree. A day out on the bay
is the best way to spend a whole afternoon together.

Bait and Tackle

We get to the store right when it opens up.
All the boats look clean and ready to be rented.
The crabbing and fishing skiffs, the big pontoons,
all the rows of single and double kayaks lined up, prepped.

This place is what we think of as "old beach."
Wally Reed is the owner and as soon as he sees my dad,
he hollers out. They're both volunteer firefighters.
Grew up on the island. They both know it
from end to end. Been here for generations.
Wally always complains about the new Hawk Marina.
He says it was set up in Manahawkin to put him out
of business and appeal to all the newbies coming in.
But the locals are loyal, and we'll never go anywhere else.

"My man, Johnny Marino. Been missing you,"
Wally calls out. "Crabbing?" he asks, clapping
my dad on the back, pulling him in for a hug.
He knows us, knows our routine. Knows
we don't have to stop here, but it's family.
Give business when we can. Stop in,
check on the people who check on us.

"Chicken necks or old fish heads today?"
Wally asks, and I have to look away while he pulls
bags of crab bait from the fridge behind the counter.

"We're gonna catch dinner for tonight," Jack says,
studying the bait and getting ready.
Crabbing is his favorite pastime
and what all of us grew up doing.

Ada and I

make our way outside
and sit on one of the picnic tables
near the boats and kayaks.
I lie down on one side,
let the morning sun wash over me,
feeling just a little bit hung over.
My eyes are closed, when all of a sudden
I hear a voice above me—a voice I recognize.

"Hi, hey—don't I know you?" he says.

I sit straight up and suddenly I see Milo
smiling right in my direction. That smile.
His jawline, his shoulders, and the way he looks
at me. I catch my breath. Ada sits up too,
staring at both of us now. Watching close.

"Eliza, right?"

"Yeah, that's right."

"Milo," he says, pointing to himself.
"We met at the beach last night."

"M i l o," Ada says, slowing the word down
and looking right at me. "Met at the beach, huh?
Good to know. So, what's your story?"

I look at her. *Stop.* "You don't have to answer that.
She was just going *back inside*
to help Dad with the bait, right?"

"Nope. I was just planning to stay right here."

"No, that's fine. I'm Milo . . ."

"Got that," Ada says, nodding.

Milo smiles at both of us. "Your sister, right?
Feels a little like I've been in this conversation
before. Yeah. So I'm seventeen," he says. Ada nods.
"And I am from the city . . . New York.
Upper East Side," he says, looking guilty.
"First summer on Long Beach Island.
Can't surf. Can hardly catch a wave,
and can't walk anywhere without flip-flops,"
he admits, pointing at his shoes.

"A newbie, huh? My folks would call you
a 'shoobie.' Someone who's just dropping in.
Where are you staying?"

"Ada, seriously? You don't have to answer
that," I explain, standing up, looking
for Dad and Jack. Ready to start this day
and get away from playing twenty questions
with my little sister. Besides, being
around Milo is making me feel nervous
in a way that I never do, and I am ready
for this feeling to disappear.

"Ship Bottom. The LBI Hotel."

"The LBI hotel? Ohhh, so fancy!
All summer? That must be really nice,"

Ada says, coming over to stand beside me,
nudging me with her elbow.
Very subtle, I think, shoving her away.

"They have some apartment-style rooms.
So longer-term stays. It's no big deal."

"It's totally a big deal. That place is high end,"
Ada says, looking at me to confirm.
"Definitely not a place for the locals.
I can say that for sure. Mom said
they have a twenty-five-dollar cocktail at the bar.
Who would even go there? Totally
for tourists," she adds.

I want to evaporate.

"Let me explain"

is what Milo says, a slight look of panic
flashing in his eyes.

"We don't live like that. It's just for the time being.
It's just while we figure out what our situation
uh . . . looks like. We're definitely not those
kind of people," he finishes,
but as soon as he does,
the car door opens on the massive black Escalade
sitting in the parking lot.

"Miloooo," the woman calls out.

Milo looks up to the sky
as if he is searching for answers.

"That's my dad . . . and my . . . stepmom,"
he says, looking at me for help.
I can't help but smile. He was not wrong.
She could definitely be his sister.
She is wearing high heels with her bathing suit
and a sarong wrapped around her waist,
her long blond hair loose down her back.

Ada looks over too. "Woooow! That is
a statement ride right there. Not so worried
about your carbon footprint, huh?" She laughs.
"That's not really in line with the Climate Justice
Seekers, so I don't know about this."

"The who?" Milo asks.

"Eliza didn't tell you about them?
CJS for short. They're basically working
to save the island from overbuilding
and reshaping the oceanfront.
They're no joke."

"Oh . . . I want to know more," Milo says,
looking right at me. "Tell me."

"Milo!"

We are interrupted by his stepmom,
her voice calling out to us.

"Aren't you going to introduce us
to your new little friends? I'm Olivia.
But most people call me Olive.
You can call me Olive."

I look up to see Milo shaking his head
just slightly, and then see his dad stride over.

"Dean," he announces. "Good to meet you,"
he says. Neither of them asks us
what our names are. I feel like a ghost.

"Dad, this is Eliza and Ada," Milo says.
He looks at us. "My dad." He gestures.
"And of course . . . Olive." He smiles right at me
this time. And I remember the nerves again.
His wide smile and deep brown eyes.

I feel like I'm losing my balance looking into them.

Sinking.

"He spoils me"

Olive says. "The biggest and the best,"
she finishes, walking over to the luxury pontoon,
the one that rents for $1,000 for half the day.
I know this because my dad points it out
every time we stop for bait. Says no one
in their right mind would spend that much
to just ride around on the bayside.
Says that's the problem with LBI these days.
Everyone treating the island like it's some
extravagant pastime. Says we need to be thankful
for nature. Not overrun it. Not overtake it.
But honor and love it. Learn to live humble
alongside it.

Milo looks at me and shakes his head.

"Pontoon boat registration?" Wally calls,
walking out with my dad and Jack.
Milo's dad and stepmom nod.
All of us stand around, taking each other in.
Waiting. Watching.

"Luxury pontoon," Dean says, reading the description
from his phone. "Plush tan seats, twenty-five feet,
brand new, deluxe as they come.
This is the one. We're meeting some friends.
Business partners," Dean explains, as if
any of us has asked him. He seems so proud of himself.

"Good luck out there"

my dad says, unfazed. He doesn't even shake his head.
Just rolls with it. He's seen this dozens of times.

"Thanks. Been thinking if we like this,
might as well buy our own someday. You own?"
he asks my dad, who has his hand up,
shading his eyes from the sunshine pushing
hard from the sky.

"Yup. That's ours right over there," my dad says,
proud of our run-down skiff that's peeling
and rusted all over. *Hail Mary, full of grace*, I start
in my head. Wishing this conversation
would end already.

Dean and Olive both look over.
Dean grins. "Well, it's good to know
you can get out on the water
in just about anything. Maybe you're the one
who needs that luck." He laughs a little this time,
as if we're all in on the joke.

Milo turns to me and mouths, *I'm sorry.*

My dad doesn't even respond. None of us do.
He just walks over, claps Wally on the shoulder,
and waves in his direction.

"To the bay," he says to all of us.
And as if the whole interaction

never happened,
we unhook our boat
and push it into the water.
Off, off, and away.

lue Claw Crabs

Scientists know them
as *Callinectes sapidus*.
In Latin, the translation is
"beautiful" (*calli*)
"swimmer" (*nectes*)
"savory" (*sapidus*).

The rules of crabbing are easy

First off, it's the Jersey Shore
and blue crabs are king. Abundant,
they swim swift through the bay.
And you can see them flash by
all olive green, blue, and red
their claws popping below.
Wait for incoming tides,
throw line traps down
and don't move too fast
give it time, go slow.
Patience wins each go.
Pull the line slow. Gentle,
easy so they rise up—
sometimes two at a time.
Hanging on to each other,
clinging. And I know it feeds us
but lately I've been wanting
to leave them alone
let them swim free and be.
Not spend all my time
catching something
that has no idea
it's being caught.

The rules of the island are harder

You grew up here. Or you didn't.

Spent all your days with sand seeping
into sheets and shoes. Tough feet
from navigating barefoot everywhere.
Learned to tell time by the tides.
Every day watching the way waves
work. Working your days around
the ocean. When to surf or ride.
Every summer soaking sunshine
Jersey Shore star-filled sky, wishing
three months could last forever.
Fishing, skim boarding, crabbing.
Peeling shrimp, grilled scallops,
cruising the boulevard, baking
on the jetty, on the pier, watching
waiting. Slow sleeping, windows
wide open to hear each crash. Salt
always in the air. May and September
supreme. When the island goes quiet
and all the full-timers can just be.

It's either you know the island
like that. Or you don't know it
at all.

We know it. That's for sure.

Catch loads of crabs. Our buckets full to the top
when we get to shore.

Dad takes his time driving us home. Takes song
requests and makes us roll the windows way down.

Air-conditioning is for the weak, we always say
as the wind blows through and in between us.

Jack closes his eyes and Ada sings loud behind me.
Dad sways in his seat and takes it all in. The way

the island tells a story—the bungalows of the past
right beside all the new money behemoth houses.

As if talking to each other, as if figuring out
how to exist together in the same place.

You can still see the damage all these years later.
Some houses just left behind. Too pricey to fix.

Forgotten and lost.

A hurricane leaves scars, all the past signs

of injury and trauma and wounds. You can see it

play out on billboards, see it in storm windows
houses that have been razed with nothing left.

Abandoned. Too weakened to revive. Lost.
That's the way some streets still look. Alone.

Disregarded. We pass Flamingo Golf, Panzone's
pizza shop, the arcade with its bells and clangs,

pass Fantasy Island and the Ferris wheel that spins,
spans the whole island. From the top—paradise.

Tourist traps and stores with history. Family spots
that stayed open after the floods and the destruction.

People who helped at all hours. Woke up ready
and went to sleep exhausted. Worked this whole place

to make it feel whole again. We wave at our neighbors
and the people who are family to us. Home to us.

But the truth is—

A scar will never fully go away.

All the time rising above—marking what once was.

Always we can feel what's just below the surface.

Beneath and shaping us all the time. This island

will always remember its endless struggle. How it rocked

beneath the rain and wind. The king tides, pools

that soaked the earth. How the ocean met the bay.

Marked by destruction. The catastrophe it cannot

shake loose. So we all lose sleep at night remembering

what this place will never forget.

The story of a family that won't quit

My family doesn't get all caught up
in the past. What went wrong
or how to fix it.
We don't wait around
for help. We do it ourselves.
Not a second of laziness
is tolerated here. We work.

My family imagines the future.
Dreams it and sees it.
Family born with Italian roots.
Then Jersey raised.
Working class.
Worked for everything we've got
and sometimes that doesn't feel like
much. But we work.

All jobs are good enough.
"You have a job, you're set,"
my dad is always saying.
He reminds us never to say,
"I have to go to work."
Reframe it. "I get to go to work.
Not everyone gets that opportunity.
Be thankful. Show up.
Let 'em know you can work
hard. Be strong. Resilient."

Work in our bones.
Work in our hearts

and lungs. Work in our bodies.
Never resting. Not stopping.

Sunup to sundown.
No one is too good to sweat.
No one is too good to get dirty.
No one is above a steady paycheck.
Hard earned. Hard won.
Calloused fingers. Aching muscles.
Dead tired at night from work,
working to the bone. Bone tired.
But paid in respect. And enough money
for a good life. A good living.
I carry that with me—always.

Family Dinner

Once we get home, it doesn't take long for our street
to fill up with bicycles and a couple of cars. Mr. Diaz
and all the kids walk over. Isa carries her art supplies,
her canvas bag spilling over. I text Zach and Mia, tell them
to pick up avocados and lime and cilantro. Tell everyone
it's the Marino Family Crab Boil. Dad and Mr. Diaz
get started on cleaning the crabs with Jack and Rio.
Our neighbors across the street who are pushing 80
come over with a cooler of shrimp dip and cold beer.
Ada, Mateo, and Marisol take turns on the hammock
and turn the speakers all the way up on the patio.
Everyone stays outside with the best view of the sunset.
Our house is bayside, but only a two-minute walk
to the ocean. We live on the most narrow part of the island.
And you can walk right out on the dock so you can dip
your toes in the water while watching the sun sink
into the earth. And every night people who grew up here
and the people who are just renting for a week or two
or the whole season, gather on that same dock. All of us
watching the wonder all together. Mom and Yara drive up
to the party—both of them shaking their heads and calling
to us. Praising our skills at catching crabs. Pulling us
into hugs and time for catching up. They take out leftovers,
sweets, and anything they couldn't sell in the afternoon.
Before long, it's a party for sure. Old Bay and lemons,
garlic sliced thin, onions and sliced potatoes, butter, parsley,
ears of corn, and a pound of smoked sausage.

"We aim to please," Dad says. We hold up our glasses
around the two picnic tables off to the side. Some of us
sit cross-legged on the rock-filled yard.

"To the start of summer," my mom calls out.

"To the tourists spending all their money
at our seafood shack!" Yara sings.

"To saving the marshland," Isa says.

"To saving our home,"
I add, hugging her to my side.

"Let's eat!" Jack yells.

Friday, July 8 | Climate Justice Seekers Meet-Up
Eight weeks to demolition . . .

"Don't ever forget it was women who saved the island,"
Yara says. My mom nods along.

We have invited them to be guest speakers for CJS
and our second meet-up of the summer.
We wanted to bring local guests
who would inspire our work.
My mom and Yara are perfect.
They are already wound up and talking nonstop.

The crowd is bigger tonight. We are getting the word out.
All the lifeguards are present, and our families too.

Mom and Yara always lead the charge.
Always activate themselves and everyone around them.
The two of them dreaming and visioning nonstop.
We have learned from the best.

"Who is going to feed and care for you? Who shows up,
rises up when it matters? It's always the women,"
my mom adds. The two of them
finish each other's sentences.

"Hey, what about us?" a few of the men call from the back.
Everyone starts to laugh.

"Yes, yes. We are thankful for you too!
Pero, we are talking about the women now.
Remember that." Yara continues.
"As many of you know, my family is from Puerto Rico.

On our island, after Irma and Maria,
the women—my people
took over the school and fed the whole town,"
she says, reminding us about all the community-run
initiatives that shot up when help did not arrive.
"Las Carolinas was saved by the women.
They are the ones who rolled up their sleeves,
said we can do this.
They cooked and fed everyone who was hungry.
That's what we do now," she finishes.

"You have to find where you are needed.
You cannot wait for other people.
You would be waiting forever," my mom adds.
"Same with this island. It was us.
It was the grandmothers. The mothers.
It was you, Isa and Eliza, who started this organization.
It was the women who saw the need and met it.
Face forward. Unafraid. Who showed up. It was us."

"We were born of this need. Born to lead this movement,
this moment," Yara says.

"It was women. I just want us all to remember that.
To hold that up and to remind you all that you can do anything.
Change anything. This world is yours.
You have to learn to take and make what is yours."

As if in sync. They both look out to the crowd.
To Isa, to me, to all our friends.

And I believe both of them. So much.

Women—what we are here for—how we show up

Women—not hurricanes. Not destructive or wrecking
anything or anyone in our path. Women—doing
the work. At all times. Women. Living out loud.
Hard & fierce. Women hungry for change. Women
arriving with help. Becoming. Showing up. Feeding.
Delivering. Bandaging. Holding. Nursing. Taking
charge & care of. I am witness to the power of women.
See the way they hold & handle it all. See it clear.
Watch them as examples. Try & follow behind them.
Every second of every day.

After the meeting

Isa and I sit outside of the schoolyard.
We can hear the ocean in the background
see the dark sky fill up with stars.
It's true, this town is sometimes sleepy
with no cars coming down the road
and no loud, late-night partying.
It's just us. Listening for the sounds
the night makes.

"I saw Milo a few days ago," I admit.

"What?" Isa asks, leaning back—looking
dead at me. "And you waited all this time
to tell me this? Did you text him?"

"No, no. Nothing like that.
We ran into him.
At the boatyard.
His family was there.
Renting a luxury pontoon.
So . . ."

"So what?" Isa asks.

"So . . . I don't know . . . they're rich.
Like really, really rich.
And he's basically LIVING
in the LBI hotel.
They drive an Escalade," I add,
rolling my eyes even though I know

Isa can't see me. I roll them for myself.
Still annoyed at the whole interaction.

"Eliza, what's the real problem?"

"I don't know," I say. Annoyed.
Embarrassed. "It just made me feel
like we were out of place. With our old
run-down boat and beat-up car.
Just felt like he belonged in the new LBI.
The one where people live in hotels
and rent fancy boats. The same people
who build those big tacky houses.
The ones who think destroying
the marshland is good for business.
That's how I felt. All those things."
I let out a breath—realize I've been
holding on to it too long.
"Felt like I was the one
who didn't fit in.
I felt lost. And I've been
thinking about it ever since."

"I get it. I do. And that is exactly
what we're fighting for.
To let people know us,
know this island.
It's what our moms
have been saying.
It's up to us.
We make the change.
We tell our story.
Milo and his family

being here, spending time on the island,
doesn't change that.
We have to live with the tourists.
They make the shack run—they make
the whole island run for three months a year.
You can't hate him for that.
But you can tell him how you feel.
You can be friends with him.
You don't have to carry that with you all the time.
Let it go, Eliza.
Don't judge him before you even know him."

I nod. Look up to keep the tears steady—
not let them fall fast. She is right. I know.
Gulp in another breath. And try to stay true
to who I am, to what I know.

At night, I catalog the disasters

keep them rumbling around inside my head.
It's what keeps me afloat and what keeps me awake.

From Puerto Cabezas to Old San Juan to Beach Haven
to New Orleans to Houston to Miami to Venice—

I know we are not in this alone. Know the world stays
engulfed in so much water. All of it rising
up around us.

Gulf
Ache
Sink

Heavy rains
Wind

Category 1
Category 2
Category 3
Category 4

Cataloging all the disaster.
This is what I have become excellent at.

Make a list of everything that was lost for us
and everything that keeps getting lost.

Every hurricane a path of destruction all around.
The insurance companies want us

to write down every single item
that was washed away.

They want us to catalog our pain.
Write it down. Make a list of everything
that doesn't exist anymore.

I catch the news. Scroll through the *Times*
and the climate section every day.

Now hurricane season seems to last
forever.
And I am cataloging it all
along the way.

What's Left

Late at night, alone on my roof,
I am all the time thinking of hurricanes.
Disaster-ology. The study of disasters.
What makes a thing break down.
Salt-watered catastrophe.
How the ocean went ahead and sank
everything in its path. Wrecking all
in its wet and reckless journey. Especially
my whole life and home and family store.
And livelihood. Legacy. I look at the stars lately
and see only pollution. A whole
New Jersey sky full of waste.
Feel wasted. The gulls flailing about
wondering how much time they've got left.
I have been wondering the same thing.
Time—and how much of it is gone.
My mom and Yara telling us to stay in,
keep fighting. Keep pushing.
Never forget. Forge a new way
out of nothing. That's what we did.
What we've been trying to do.
But I feel like I am just treading water
just staying afloat myself.
Just barely
breathing.

If I talk about it enough, will anything
change? If I obsess over sea levels
and temperatures and how the water
continues to

rise

      rise

         rise

will anything at all

   change?

These Days

I am trying desperately to stay
in the now, but looking
fast at the future
at the exact same time.
Trying to stay rooted
and keep growing
but not look back.
And lately, I am feeling
attached but flailing.
Trying to hang on
but losing my grip.
Every day I wake up
remembering how lucky I am
how lucky we all are
to still be here,
breathing and alive.

I look at Jack and Ada
who are always
still asleep when I wake
and I am thankful
for their soft breathing
and the covers pulled up,
just the three of us still.

Each morning I rise
without waking them.
Comfort in knowing
they will sleep
through my worry.

Things my therapist says—

Talk it out. Find the thread and pull it loose.
Don't let your thoughts take over your mind.
You must let it all out. Write it down.
Share it with a friend. Don't keep it all
bottled up, weighing you down. You
are stronger than you realize.

Monica is no nonsense. She does not
let up. Or let me get away with short
or simple answers. She is relentless.
Takes up space with her questions.
Stays upfront with me. Reminds me
that I am not alone. Talks about her own
relationship to storms. To disasters.
Growing up in Miami. She knows
the story of disappearing islands.
Shares her family history
her roots from Ghana and Mississippi.
Says Black and Brown communities
are in this too. Doing the work.
All of us connected.
Echoes my mom and Yara
and how they are all the time saying
This is collective.
That to see yourself is to see everyone.
To see the community around us.
Knowing this is an always reminder
to replace *I* with *we*. We are in this.
Together.

So cool and laid back that I want
to make her proud. Sits across from me,
her glasses tilted down. Her short hair
cut close. Earrings hugging her neck.
She is all the time confident in who she is
and all that she has been through.
I pay close attention.
Want to be that calm myself. Been seeing her
since the hurricane. Since my counselor
at school thought I needed more
than she could handle.

Monica lives in Philly,
but comes to LBI once a week.
She works with those of us
who are still struggling with loss.
Still figuring out how to wade through.
Calls it trauma-informed care.
Calls it the four R's: Realization.
Recognizing the signs. Having a system
to Respond. And Resisting re-traumatization.

She is no nonsense about care.
About her patients. About me.

Questions Monica asks—

What are you afraid of?
What does being free mean to you?
What does liberation mean to you?
How can you get it?
What do you want to be liberated from?
Who is responsible for you?
How can you switch from surviving
to thriving?
What does that look like to you?
How can you switch from thought
to action?

Activations Monica suggests—

All this stress and anxiety can hold you back.
Take deep breaths. Go on long walks.
Don't forget to meditate. Sweat.
Go for that run you're always talking about.
Surf all those monster waves.
Fill your life. Face the ocean.
Do it for your family.
Do it for yourself.

The other side of the story, is . . .

I never thought
I was a kid
who'd go
to therapy.

Never imagined
my mind
would hold on to
so much fear
that it kept me
from
falling
asleep.

Didn't know
trauma
stays.

Or that I'd have to fight
to shake it loose.

But every single
time we talk.
I can feel
my mind
start to unhinge.
Untangle itself.

I am not ashamed
of asking for help.
I am not scared

of the pain
anymore.

Just more ready
to face it
dismantle it
break it down
reveal it
for what it is
and try to destroy it
before it
destroys
me.

But sometimes

it feels like
that fight
is just
beginning.

Everything Changes

This, I know. What is settled becomes wrecked.
What is safe becomes panic. What is imagined
becomes real. Home is a distant memory.
Unless you have lived it, waded through it,
searched the water for something that you loved,
then you could never ever know. What is loss?
Hungry ocean and all it takes away.
How to love something that could end you.

Every morning, I take to the beach. Grab a towel,
throw on a bathing suit, no shoes, no bag. Nothing
else between me and the waves. Walk the two minutes
from my front door to the roar. At night, I can hear
each crash of each wave. The way it calls to me. Soothes
my panic but was part of it too. When it feels like
it has taken me years to get over my fear, I remember
that it has. This salt is a part of me too. My home.

Each time is like the first. No lifeguard on duty at nine a.m.,
but I can save myself. Never tell my folks I go in. Lie
and say I am always careful. But every morning, I wade out
way past my waist and then to my shoulders. I cannot
be afraid anymore. That is the lie I have been telling myself.
Dunk under, let it wash me, over me, pull up beside me.
The tides draw me out and back again. Do not resist. Do
not pull away. Do not panic. Never panic. Do not fear
nature or the sea. Do not remember the past. Think only
of the future. Breathe. When you hold your breath, believe
that you can let it go. That you will come back up for air.

Surfing on Holyoke

I see him again.
Standing on the shoreline.
Milo Harris.
His whole name sounds private school.
It sounds slacks and ties to dinner.
Sounds country club. SUV.
Sounds financial planning and second home.
Sounds trust fund and never had to work a day
in his whole life. It sounds inheritance and wealth to me.

I study him from my surfboard.
My perch, place to watch and figure out the next move.
His board is brand new. Shining.
I can see how expensive it is all the way
from the middle of the ocean.
That is how rich I am sure he is.

Zach and Mia—who I am now certain
are full-on traitors—stand beside him.
I stop to let the ocean rise up and over me a few times.
Dunk underneath and then come up.
Salt, salt everywhere.

Who does he think he is?

They wave me in and I dunk underneath one last time
and then walk slow to the shore.

"Found You"

This is what Zach says, waving me in,
tilting their head in my direction.

"Well, it is where I surf every afternoon, so . . ."

"So, we are genius detectives," Zach says.

"I . . . hi, again," I say.

"Hey. It's my fault. Totally on me. I saw them
at the wharf and we started talking about surfing
and my nonexistent skills and they just said . . ."

"That I'd help?"

Milo looks at Zach and Mia like he's in a trap.
When truthfully, it's me who's the one
that's been set up.

"I just . . . need all the help I can get"

Milo says. And somehow him just saying those words,
just admitting it, makes me like him,
A little bit. Kind of. I can't tell,
but when he takes his shirt off,
I feel warm all over
and can't tell where to look.

Mia looks at me, looks at Milo's chiseled body,
looks back at me and raises her eyebrows.
As if to say, *Do you see what we mean?*
And I do.

Do not be superficial, I think to myself.

"We'll help too," Zach says, holding their board
and prepping to go in the water.
"Come on," Mia says, pulling my arm.
"Let's just catch a few waves. It'll help you
feel free," she says, and tugs me along.

She is wearing my favorite bathing suit
with cutouts all over it, showing off
her body, which she is never
afraid to do.

I feel powerful beside her. Both of us,
strong and tough from so much surfing
pushing off and sprinting to the ocean,
ready to feel the salt again
on our skin.

Take two . . . take three . . .

Milo struggles behind us, his board
clunky next to him. It's clear
he's an athlete, but definitely
not one with the ocean.

He can't get past the waves,
so they barrel him, push
past and over him.

Finally, he makes it
to us. Out of breath
exhausted.

"Maybe surfing is not for me," he says.

All of us are straddling our boards
but he looks like he's hanging on
for dear life. Holding on
with his upper body
while his legs
kick below.

"You mean you're already giving up?"
I ask, teasing him now. It's not every day
that I get to teach someone a new trick
a new way to be in the world.
Not to say I know exactly,
but this
I am good at.
This,
I understand.

"No, no! Not giving up, just maybe
rethinking my strategy. Is there
even a strategy in surfing?"

"Of course. But really,
you have to listen to the waves,
become . . . a wave whisperer
if you will," Zach says,
winking while looking behind,
paddling out farther
and catching the first wave
of the afternoon.

"You have to feel it," Mia
adds. Even though
she just started surfing
she knows exactly
how to wait
for a wave.

She takes the next wave in,
and then it's just the two of us.
Floating. Rocking.
Trying to stay above.

How to Ride

"They're right," I say.
"It's just about instinct.
Balance," I add, moving
my board closer to him.
I hold his steady, tell him
to be patient. Go slow
as he eases his body
on top to sit. And then
we're face-to-face.
The sun washing over
both of us. The ocean
slow and steady beneath.
"Feel it. You can watch
for it." Put my palms
to the water. As it floats
me up, then down.
"You want to catch
the wave just as it rises,
just as it pulls up,"
I say, looking out,
remembering to stop
being afraid. Pushing
myself to believe
the ocean does not
want to hurt me,
or us. "Soon as it rises
you have to paddle,
fast as you can,
to get under it
before it crashes
before it washes away.

If you do that
you can ride it
for what feels like
forever."

Time Out

"So, just to be clear, no one
catches a wave the first time out,
right?" Milo asks, lying out
flat on his back, clearly exhausted.

"No, definitely not," Zach says,
eyeing me. "Except Mia did.
She caught a lot of waves.
And Isa and Eliza too.
I mean, they were practically born
surfing. So they did."

"And Zach too. Totally caught a bunch
the first time," I add. All of us
laughing now. At Milo's expense.
But he seems to like it, so it feels good.
Good to be laughing, good to be together.
Good to feel loose and free.
"You weren't that bad!"

"I wasn't that good though, either."
He sits up and looks directly at me.
"But you're a good teacher.
I took notes . . . in my head."

"Good. Keep going over them.
Really, all you have to do
is be like Keanu Reeves
in *Point Break*. That's the game,"
I say, high-fiving Zach,
who has their hand ready

soon as I bring up
our all-time favorite
surfing movie.
Legend, since
our parents
introduced it to us.
Made us watch it.
Made us love it.

"Never seen it," Milo says.
And all of us stare straight at him
and jump to our feet.

"What!?" Mia asks. "You cannot
even begin to surf without seeing it."

"Wait, wait, wait," I start in.
"You've never seen *Point Break*?
I kind of need you to leave the beach
right this second,
go home, watch it,
and then—report back.
Because that is the ULTIMATE
surfing movie. The only way to go.
You got Keanu Reeves and Lori Petty.
He would be nowhere without her.
Her skills, her know-how,
her basic brilliance on the waves.
There. That's your lesson right there.
I can't do anything else for you
until you watch that movie."

We stay steady looking at him.
"Oh, you all are serious?" he asks,
suddenly standing up himself.

"Totally and completely serious,"
I say, smiling wide at him now.

He starts to laugh, picks up his bag,
looks at me for a second longer
and then grabs his surfboard.
"I'm on it. For you . . . anything."

"Oh, and leave that fancy board home
the next time. I'll let you borrow
one of mine. One that's been worn in."

"Next time?" he asks. "So,
there's gonna be a next time?"

"Somebody's gotta teach you,"
I say as he walks backward away,
returning my smile the whole time.

"Ohhhhhhh . . . you like him"

Zach says as soon as he's off the beach.
All of us looking in his direction.

"Somebody likes him," Mia sings.

"Shut up! Both of you. I do not like him
like that. Also this whole thing was a total
and complete setup. You're the worst friends ever.
Isa would never have done this to me."

"Yeah . . . too bad she had her lifeguard shift
and just couldn't stop us." Mia laughs.

"He's a good guy," Zach says, shrugging their shoulders.
"I'm just saying. We've hung out a few times
and he's cool. And he likes you."

"How do you even know he's a good guy?
What does that even mean?
You don't know his family,
you don't know what he—"

"Eliza, I'm not saying you have to marry the guy.
I'm just saying he's not as bad
as you're trying to make it. That's all."

"Fine. I'll help him surf. I'm good with that.
Anyway . . . how do you know he likes me?"
And as soon as the question comes out of my mouth
I regret it, because they both start to ohh and ahh
at me. Singing about how much I like Milo.

"You like him. Admit it," Zach says,
grabbing our bags as we pack up to leave too.
"I just want to hear it. Out loud."

"Fine. And if I admit it, will you both
stop bothering me already?"

They both stop walking and look right at me.

"I like him . . . a little bit."

Maybe a lot. Maybe I couldn't stop looking at him
treading water. Floating beside me.
But they don't have to know that. Just yet.

Friday, July 15 | Climate Justice Seekers Meet-Up
   Seven weeks to demolition . . .

Zach and Mia start the big group meeting this week.
They pass around sign-up sheets
so everyone can figure out how to be involved.

"We have a beach clean-up planned this month.
Our end-of-summer clambake is set for September,
and so is our action against the destruction
of Clam Cove Reserve."

As soon as Zach says it, the crowd starts to clap.
There are 38 of us in the meeting this afternoon.
The sun is starting to go down outside
and we're sitting in one of our old elementary school
classrooms. It's like a one-room schoolhouse
and most of us in this room have known each other
since we were kids.

We didn't start out calling ourselves climate activists,
but that's what we are. We have gotten more comfortable
with that label.

"We have some choices to make," Mia says,
calling everyone to attention.
"We want to make a statement.
Get people to listen up, pay attention.
On the day of demolition, what do we want to do?"

We want to protest!

Host a sit-in.

A day of action to stop
the Hope/Hart Construction project.

I hear *yes* and *come on* and *that's right*
coming from the crowd.

Everyone has ideas. And the energy feels alive
and the movement feels real.

"Good. I love this," Zach says.
"Now let's get to work."

Our Partners

Since the start of Climate Justice Seekers
we have worked hard to partner across the island
from Barnegat Light to Holgate
and every small town in between.

Loveladies, Harvey Cedars, North Beach,
Surf City, Ship Bottom, Beach Haven

We ask people want they need and want.
What stays on their minds?
What does it mean to get involved?

The Long Beach Island Foundation
of Arts + Sciences
is one of our long-term partners.
Protecting and teaching
about the ecology of LBI.
From them, we've learned
about the ocean, dunes,
salt marshes, the mud flats and bay.
All the wildlife that surrounds us.
Laughing gulls, crabs, and starfish.
And all the habitats too.
Beach zones, maritime forests,
and coastal dunes. The salt marsh
we're working to protect.
All of it feels impermanent
and like it could slide
between our fingers
if we are not careful.

So we pay attention to the science.
Keep everyone off the dunes,
work to replant where we can,
promote alternative energy,
fight for island-friendly legislation,
clean up all our trash from the beaches,
don't throw anything in the ocean,
and most of all, spread the word.
Get everyone involved to help us
preserve this place.

Environmental Stewardship

We understand now
what that really means.
And how to uphold the values
that our families
and our elders
and those who came before us
were all about.
We listen
all the time now.

On the way home

Zach rides close beside me
and asks if I'm okay.

"You were a little quiet tonight."

"Just taking it all in," I say.
"Every week, more people show up.
It's like this little club we started after the hurricane
and every year we did a little more. Shared our stories,
talked about the island. And all of a sudden,
it feels like we're making things happen,
like we could actually make a difference."

"That's right!" Zach shouts. Calling out
into the fading blue sky. "We did this. This was us.
I keep thinking about the fact that it's not just us
on our little island. It's everywhere.
Puerto Rico and New Orleans.
Bangladesh and Manila and Panama.
We are in this together.
Water and the risk
of rising tides.
It's everywhere.
And the more we talk about it
and the more noise we make
the better."

So that's what we do.
Start to shout
and holler
and get rowdy

standing up
on our bikes
and shouting
together
toward
the setting
sun.

Surf Is All the Way Up

"I watched it. I watched it three times. I'll watch it again.
Anything for you to teach me how to be like Keanu,"
Milo says when we see each other the next day.

And the day after that and the day after that and the day . . .

We meet on Holyoke most of the time. Between
Glendola and Iroquois. Best surfing on the whole island.

The jetties helping to break up the currents. Rip tides
strong between here and Nelson Avenue. We ride.
Every day this week. Spending half the time in the water
and the other half sitting leaned against the dunes.
Each afternoon warm on the sand.
My skin heating up from the sunshine.
Talking about the waves, talking about staying above
and how to wrestle with the sea. I can't tell what he wants
more: to know me or to know the water. Both of us
some of the time hard to follow. He is learning to read
the ocean, how it can tease and shake you awake.

He is starting to read me too. Every day. We are starting
to talk more than we surf. Telling each other everything
there is to know.

You Go First

"Favorite food?" Milo asks.

"Clams with just a little hot sauce.
And my mom's crab cakes. Hands down."

"Song on the playlist of your life?"

"Wow. That one's deep," I say.
"'New Rules' by Dua Lipa."

"Good choice," he says.
"Three things you can't live without?"

"My family. The ocean. Surfing."

"What about me?"

I laugh. "We just met. I don't know you
like that yet."

"Okay, I can accept that. Maybe
I'll be added to the list," he says.
"I got another. Favorite candy as a kid?"

"Jolly Ranchers. You?"

"Chocolate. Anything," he adds.

I smile. "Swimming or snowboarding?"
I ask, knowing his answer already.

"Definitely snowboarding. But lately
I think I could love surfing. Maybe?"

"Definitely," I answer. "Once you get it."

"Wait, are you saying
I still haven't gotten it?"

"I mean . . . I'm just trying to tell the truth."

He falls backward in the sand,
laughing at himself. At this situation.
At me. At us sitting below the dunes
learning everything there is to know.

Some of the time

we just swim, just let the water wash right over us.
And sometimes we just sit right where the waves crash
bury our feet in the sand cool and easy and cresting over.

We talk about living on the island and he asks endless
questions about how we grew up, what we love,
what we'd miss if we had to leave. I tell him
since the hurricane, I am always packing my bags,
always thinking about who to protect, what to carry
with me if I have to outrun a storm.
Think about what to save—if anything at all,
or what to leave behind.
How much can you carry with you?
On your back? In the car?
On a trip far away?
What can you live without?
That kind of damage can mark you.
Can make you lose sleep, lose clarity,
lose parts of your mind you thought were safe.

I say it all without thinking.
Somehow his questions
make me remember.
Make me see my life
the way it was.
Not the way it is.

WHAT TO LEAVE BEHIND

FIVE YEARS AGO

Unforgiving Questions

What would you carry with you?
    What would you leave behind?

Is this the end of the world as we know it?
    How do we survive the end of the world?

What will be left when we return?
    What will we even return to?

Who will be left alive?
    What will be left standing?

Can we ever come back?
    What will be lost?

How can we return?
    If there is nothing left?

Endless

Panic sets in.
Wind whips wild
outside our door.
No electricity now.
Nowhere to hide.
Nothing to protect.
We gather together
and say we will never
let go. Arms linked.
Hustle around.
So loud
we can't hear
or think
our thoughts
jumbled.
All of us
crying now
and can't help
myself.
Can hear
the rush
of water
outside.

"It's time to leave!"

My dad yells.
We have made the mistake
of staying too long.

Our car just outside
just within reach
of an exit.

Grab backpacks
and stuff anything
everything.

My whole life
is flashing
wild around me.

Outside the window
is water and loss
fear wrapping.

Grab sweatshirt
and socks, shoes
and toothbrush.

I am forgetting
something
everything.

Pack for Jack
and Ada. Pull
clothes, jackets.

"The shack," my mom
moans. Her life's
work—sinking.

"We have to go,"
my dad shouts
all of us—a rush.

Breath

     Loose

   Shake

Ache

   Moan

Cry

     Whisper

   Crash

Wave

     Awake

Alert

   Lose

     Breathe

   Shout

Shout

   Shout

     Drown

Air

    Shook

        Late

Rage

        Ocean

    Bay

        Flood

Fast

Outside is heavy

flooding. Lose my footing.
We run.

The water rushes past us,
soaks my shoes and feet.

Drenched all over.
Mom and Dad tell us to run
get to the car. And fast.

We try. I am only twelve.
Ada is ten. Jack is six.
I am in charge.

We rush. Ocean and bay
pushing up around us
fast, fast, fast.

No way we can leave,
no way we stay
hurry.

Can't keep up. Can't
hold my ground.
Lose Jack's hand.

He stumbles loose
from my grip, gets caught
in the tide.

That is pushing us.
The street already full
of waves and salt.

Swirling and ripping
around us. He falls
in the water.

I scream his name
Jack!
Jack!

Tell Ada to hold on
to the car door
and not move.

My dad runs
outside,
hears me screaming.

Jack tumbling, turning
his arm waving
us to him.

He keeps losing
balance
lost in the water.

My heart is sink
sinking
in my chest.

The tides twisting
and turning him
pushing his body.

He can swim
but is struggling
dunking under.

Again
and
again.

All I see is my brother disappearing—

Only to appear. Again.
How do I go deep without drowning?
Grab for his arm, his legs
anything to hold on.
I am reaching, reaching.
He is sinking, sinking.

"Dad!" I holler. "Help! Now!"

"Are you okay?"

I shake out of it when Milo puts his hand
on my shoulder, concerned.

"I lost you for a second," he says.
"You were sitting right here,
but it seemed like your mind
was somewhere else."

I do not tell him that my flashbacks
still take me out. Still remind me
when I am most trying to forget.
Still get my heart racing
tipping, turning inside me.
Shaking all of me apart.

Post-traumatic stress disorder. Water
stress. Water risk. Risk of damage.
Risk of exposure. Risk of heartbreak.
If you feel your heart opening
and then see it closing
right back up.
That is a sign
you are not okay
my therapist
is always
saying.

I take a few quiet breaths. Breathing
in and out. Fill my lungs up to capacity.
Think of rolling with the tides.

The way I was taught as a kid.
Don't fight it. Don't wrestle
the ocean. You will lose
every time.

Remain Calm

Steady the beat. Steady my breathing.
Steady my ability to adjust.
To calm. To rally.
To let go.

As soon as I get my heart
to slow down, Milo puts his hand
over mine. And holds on.

And just like that.
My heart starts to speed up,
racing and flying outside
of my chest.

"I miss New York"

he says, one afternoon.
We are the only ones left on the beach.
Both of us staying late—watching the sky
lose its color. "And my mom.
I miss her too."

"She's back in the city?" I ask, realizing
that we haven't talked about our families
at all. There is so much I don't know
about him. And so much he doesn't know
about me. My past—what I think about
for the future.

"Yeah, she stayed. It's us that left. My dad
does pretty much everything my stepmom
wants him to do. So, we're here.
Just for the summer, but it feels like a lot.
To live with my dad and his new wife
to be in this new place I've never been.
And the real truth is . . . I don't think
I'm cut out for island life," he finishes,
leaning back on his arms. I lean back too,
join him lying out in the sand.
Our arms just barely touching
and it feels like electricity running
straight through me, from the top
of my head to the bottom of my toes.
Electric. Warm waves all over.
The sea inside of me.

"Wow," I say, suddenly realizing
I am talking out loud.

"I know," he replies, clearly not seeing
how I seem to be falling apart beside him.
"My mom keeps saying I need to
give it a chance. Learn to love all this,"
he adds pointing at the sea. "This helps,"
he says, looking at me and my surfboard.

"Yeah, I can help," I assure him.
Nodding my head, standing and looking out
over the water. At the houses in the distance.
"I can definitely help. Let me show you.
I'm gonna make you love this island.
If it's the only thing I do this summer.
Gonna prove to you that ocean living
is the absolute best kind of living.
The only kind of living. When I'm done
with you, you'll be like: New York what?
I don't even know that place. You won't
even miss the city for a second."

He smiles. A smile I am starting to get used to.
"Well then prove it," he says. "I'm all yours."

Hometown

"So I have to make a list of places to go
and things we can do. I mean, I feel like
I should show him the real island, you know?
The one that the tourists *don't* get to see.
Our home. So I got the lighthouse down,
Flamingo Golf, because . . . classic.
And Geno's for Philly cheesesteaks,
a drive down through Loveladies,
the Ferris wheel—just to see the island
from up above, uh . . . Surf's Up Books
in Ship Bottom, a tour of Cedar Bonnet,
kayaking in Manahawkin Bay, uh . . . what else?"

I look up and everyone is staring at me. Hard.
Mia and Isa are sprawled out on the floor
in my bedroom, and Zach is sitting
on the bottom bunk. Looking dead at me.

"I'm sorry. Can you just rewind? Back it up
juuusssttt a little bit," Zach says, sitting up
and hitting their head on the top bunk.
"What. Are. You. Talking. About?"

"What? It is so not a big deal. I was just
talking about a tour—just a basic . . . you know . . .
introduction to the island, that's all. No big . . ."

"Uhh, very big deal. You're talking about
ten-fifteen DATES is what you're talking about.
With Milo. Harris, that is. Your boyfriend."

"Clearly," Isa adds. "So, you want us to help you
pick out the perfect things to wear?" She gets up,
starts to look through my closet. All of us
know there's nothing new at all in there.
But she pulls out my favorite jeans
and my most worn-in flip-flops
and the tank top that fits me
perfectly. My silver hoops
she lays out on the dresser.
"I know you're always
gonna do what you want,
but I'd wear this.
And your green army jacket
from the Salvation Army.
Classic beach you," she finishes.

Zach pulls my makeup bag
from the shelf. "And maybe
just a little of this."
They all smile in my direction.
Knowing I am in this
deeper than I thought.

How to go deep—without drowning.

I am still trying to figure that out.

Island Dreaming

"So let me get this straight. You're gonna give me a tour?
Of the whole island? Seventeen miles? On a bicycle?"

"What? Are you . . . scared? Are you . . . wait a minute . . .
can you ride a bike? Do I need to teach you that too?"

"No, I . . . of course I can ride a bike. I just . . .
I did grow up in New York City, so . . .
I'm not like 100 percent on two wheels.
I could drive us," he says, looking at me, motioning out
to the Escalade sitting in my driveway.
It looks as big as our entire house.
I say nothing, then shake my head when Ada and Jack
come out of the front door
as if they could sense I was about to go on a date.
Even though I'm not officially using that word.

"Well look who it is," Ada says,
parking it on the steps outside our house.

Jack runs over to high-five Milo.
They met again a few days ago at the beach.

"You remember my sister, Ada, and my brother, Jack.
Jack, Ada—you remember Milo."

"Of course we do. So catch us up.
Where are you taking him today?
On my cruiser, I might add," Ada asks,
seeing that I have dragged her old bike
out from the shed.

"Is that even safe?" Milo asks,
eyeing the bike and then me.

"Maybe you should take it slow today.
Just ride up to The Boardwalk for ice cream and . . ."

"Take him to the park," Jack adds.
"They have the best and highest swings
over on West Avenue."

"Okay, could you two maybe
go somewhere else? Anywhere else?"
I ask, steadying Ada's bike and handing it to Milo.
"I got this.
We got this."
"Have fun," Ada calls to us,
both she and Jack waving goodbye.

"Did your brother and sister
just plan our whole afternoon?"
Milo calls out, rushing to catch up.

"No," I say, stopping at the corner.
I pause, start to think about the plan
and realize Ada and Jack are right.
Maybe staying local is better
than riding the seventeen miles
all the way to Barnegat Light
with someone who can hardly
stay upright. "Actually, yes," I say.
"I think they did."

Milo laughs and follows behind me

At the ice cream shop, he orders
two scoops of cotton candy
and I get a double chocolate fudge.
We walk to the playground
and finish while pushing up and back
on the swing set. I feel like a kid.
It's just us since everyone else
is at the beach, so we take advantage.

Swing as high as we can—our legs
pumping and flying into the air. Breeze
rushing past and over us. He sings
off tune and as loud as his voice will go.
We play tag around the jungle gym,
up and down the pirate ship
and through the makeshift rocks.
Seesaw and a race to the look out
on top. He does ten pull-ups
and I match him and then do five more.

"Show-off," he calls out. "Come on!"

"It's those surfing muscles," I brag.

"Fine. You win. I'm already liking
it here. More and more," he says,
finally catching up to me
on top of the slide.

"I'm just getting started," I say
before sliding away from him.

And then it's just us

and then we just go.

Every day after work
we meet. He comes by
with subs or I bring
leftovers from our place.
Grab ice cream
or Italian ice,
coffees from the wharf
or down Slurpees
from the 7-Eleven.
We catch the whole
island. Every night.

Mostly we cruise.
Take the boulevard
and ride. No hands
I stand while coasting.
Sail around and past.
All the time—this high
of being together
with nowhere to go
and nowhere to be.

Cruise

        slow
                hands
                        soar
                easy
        slow
ride
        high
                day
                        turn
                go
        slow
easy
        ride
                sand
                        coast
                wave
        blur
want
        memorize

                jump
                        blur
warm
        heat
                heart
                        race

                home
        night

dreaming

   more
      forever

All of a sudden

I really do want to show him
the whole island. From Barnegat Bay
to the Wildlife Refuge, all the inlets
and jetties that rise up in the tide.
Ride the Dragon and Pirate's Ship
up, up, up over the bay. Sunlight,
sunset. Dipping and heart in mouth.
Want to win rounds of miniature golf
hole in one, trophy on the last round.
Want to show off, show out for him.
Climb the steps to the lighthouse,
go crabbing, go boating, fishing
show him how to catch and release.
Want to swim late night, plankton
shimmering on top of us. Skin and sink.
Want to kiss his skin after a day
sinking beneath the water.
Want to hold him around the waist
and ride each wave to the shore.
Let the ocean kick us beneath
and below. I want him. To show him
what it means to love something
that could disappear. To love a place
where the sea level is rising so high
we could be below it. Want to hold
my breath under water, keep it,
and come up gasping for air, for him.
Taste the salt on his skin.
This is new, a fresh feeling
I am grappling with

wrestling with,
aching inside with.

It's true—he stays on my mind now
more than I had planned.

"You know I'm starting to love it here too"

Milo says. And I believe him. The way he stays
asking questions about this place. Wants to know
as much as possible.

"I know I'm not from here like you and your friends.
But I like the idea of putting down roots.
Building something up. Making a kind of history
in a place that you weren't born into.
You know, there's some work
my family is doing on the island.
Some projects my dad has been working on.
He's got ideas about how to make this place
even better for the people who live here
and the people just visiting."

I nod along, because the more time I spend with Milo
the more I want him here. The more I want to know
who he is, what he dreams about, what stays
on his mind.

"I love the way you talk about the ocean, surfing.
It's like you have this energy out on the water,
like you can only see the waves. And you're in it.
You get this look in your eyes and this focus.
You, Zach, Mia, and Isa are so . . .
I don't know . . . driven.
Like you know what you want
and you know how to get it.
I don't know anyone like you.
Like this.
The way you show up every day. Ready.

That's how I feel when I'm with you.
You make me want to show up.
You make me want to stay here
and make my own story."

I smile. Don't want him to stop talking.

Becoming Local

"I want to know more," I say, despite myself.
Despite the fact that his money
makes me feel nervous and out of place.
His car, his family living in a hotel for the summer,
his luxury everything.
I can't stop imagining the size of his new house
and how much of the beachfront it will take up
and how much his family has
for him to be living in a hotel
while building a mansion on our island.
I have stuck this knowledge deep
in the back of my mind.

But I can't stop myself. I go deeper.
Want to know more.

"I get your love for this place. I do.
And it makes me think about how I can help.
I wanna help. I wanna be part of the solution."

"Me too," I say.

"Then maybe I could come with you
to the next CJS meeting?
I heard Zach say it's open to everyone. Is it?"

And when he asks that, I realize
that I am not exactly sure who Milo Harris is,
and not sure how much of me I want to reveal.

"Oh, yeah, definitely. But really, it's no big deal," I lie.
"It's mostly for locals."

"Yeah, but I'm kind of gonna be local," he adds.

Every time I feel myself getting closer to Milo
I pull back. Realize there have got to be boundaries
for locals and tourists to exist together.
For those of us who stay
and those of us who always go away.

But I'm also falling for him
at the exact same time.

Friday, July 22 | Climate Justice Seekers Meet-Up
Six weeks to demolition . . .

I do not invite Milo.
I do not tell Zach, Mia, and Isa
that I am falling for someone
who could be standing against
what we are fighting for.

Because I am unsure of the truth.
Because my fear of drowning is back.
Because I get lost every time I look into Milo's eyes.
And forget who I am and what I care about.
Because at every meeting, I realize
how much time is slipping away.
And suddenly I want to fall in love
just as much as I want to save the island.
And I am torn.
Wrecked.
Feeling my own heart
demolished too.

Is this what love
is capable of?

Undone is how I feel.
But I push on.

Prep Work

"Eliza, did you and Isa secure vendors?"
Mia asks. Everyone already working
when I arrive. "Come on, join the group.
We're already plotting out table locations
and where everything will get set up.
We need your creative eye."

I jump in. Take Milo out of my mind.
Try and concentrate on the moment.

"Flyers are posted all over," Zach says
once I sit down in our small working group.
"And I have updates on all our social media.
I am posting something every day,
a connection to Clam Cove Reserve.
I made a whole bunch of photos,
some of the turtle nests and even more
out toward the bay. I wanna give people
a sense of this place. Want them to see it too."

"You know it's all about the turtles for us,"
Mia says, looking through Zach's images.

Isa nods as we scroll and look at the headlines.

Help us protect 24 acres of coastal marshland

Natural Habitats United

Northern Diamondback Terrapins | Help Them Nest!

Help Us Shelter

WARNING: Critical Habitat Site

Terrapins—Species of Special Concern on the Jersey Shore
JOIN US IN OUR FIGHT TO SAVE THEM

Even More

"It's about the turtles for me too," Isa starts,
"But it's even more about changing the landscape
with no real worry about what that means
in the long run."

"We want to change the narrative," I say,
remembering the point of this.
Reminding myself why we are here
and why it matters that we stay
and take up this fight.

"I am writing updates too," Isa adds.
"Making sure we share
what the marshland means
to those of us who have lived
right beside it all our lives."

"Yeah," Zach adds.
"If someone can destroy this so easily,
what else could they do?
What else would they be capable of?"

None of us wants to find out.
So we keep working.
Keep posting and sharing.
Keep spreading the word.

The Next Day

We meet outside on the wharf.

"You can come to the next meeting," I lie,
knowing there are barriers, borders
I am setting up. Don't want him
in this fight somehow. "Come on,
we're meeting the crew at Bay Village
for the best pizza in the Northeast.
You know everybody brags about New York
pizza, but the true food lovers know
that New Jersey is where it's at."

I pull him along. Zach, their friend Adam, and Isa
are all sitting on the picnic tables outside.
Milo checks in with everyone
and Zach introduces Milo to Adam,
who is grinning at both of us
in a way that suggests Zach
has told him everything.
They've already ordered two large pies
and we eat fast and order French fries
and root beers to wash it all down.

"I think I'm starting to get it.
The best beaches. The best pizza,
the best surfing, wave riding. The best
crabbing. The best people. You have it all."

"Yes, you're starting to get it," I say.

Thundering Surf

We go to meet Mia at the water park
just across the street. She's closing up.
Her dad is the manager,
so they're both staying a little late.

As soon as we get to the front, Mia's dad
lets us all in. Says they still have about half an hour.
Mr. Nash is a volunteer firefighter
so we know them like family too.
The whole town in this fight together.
He says hello to us and asks
if we want ice cream bars—on him.

This is what I want Milo to see too.
How much this place is a family—
everyone who knows you looks out for you.
Cares about you. Watches your back.

"How was yesterday's climate meeting?"
Mr. Nash asks. "Any new plans for the clambake?
Bands? DJs? Did you decide anything?"

"The clambake? When's that?" Milo asks,
looking right at me.

"End of summer. Eliza didn't tell you?
You might just make it," Zach answers.
"Best clams. Best party. Best people."

"These amazing kids are raising money
to stop this island from going under,"

Mr. Nash says, patting Zach on the back.
"Proud of you all. This place is for us.
We gotta protect it." Then he looks at Milo.
"Who are you? Do I know you?"

"No, I'm new here this summer.
They've been showing me around.
Nice to meet you," Milo says,
shaking hands with Mr. Nash.

"Good. Good. These kids are family," he says,
talking us up. "You all have been working
so hard all afternoon. You wanna take a few slides
while I shut down?" he asks us.

In This Together

"Uhhh, *yeah* we do," I say. All of us still
in bathing suits—practically living in them
this time of year. The water park
is one of the best ways to cool down.

I take Milo by the hand to show him
how it works. We climb the stairs
all the way to the top and on the lookout
you can see Fantasy Island, the calm of the bay,
the school where we all went to elementary
and where we now meet up for climate meetings,
and all the stores along the boulevard.

"You're gonna love this," I say
and guide him to the first slide.

And that's how we find ourselves
spending sunset sliding and rushing
past each other. The water riding
us down. We scream and holler
roll and fly from slide to slide.
Mia stays at the top to direct us
whirling from the fastest slide
to the one that goes slow,
then speeds up at the end.

There is a pause and jump
just before each slide ends at the pool
and my heart is jump, jumping in my chest
feeling the adrenaline kick in.
Milo and I go down two slides together.

My back against his chest
and I can feel his heart
thumping against me.
And think maybe
he is feeling
the same way
about me.

And so I forget my fears
for as long as it takes
to hold on to
this.

The next night

is fish tacos
with guacamole and chips
and red beans and rice
all at El Swell
the best Mexican food
on the whole island.
We sit outside
order watermelon
and cantaloupe aguas frescas.
Milo closes his eyes
with every bite
and I know I've got him
have made him hungry
for this place
for this life.

Miniature golf at Flamingo

is next. The oldest and most
old-fashioned of the courses,
it still reminds me
of being a kid and playing
with my family
with my friends.
All the hot pink birds
on every surface,
the potted flowers
and wooden houses
around each hole.
We compete for each round
and he beats me every time.

"See, golf is my sport. Not surfing."

"Golf is for rich kids and snobs,"
I say. He puts his hand over his heart
and looks hurt.

"Just kidding. Fine.
You're good at this. I can admit that."

"Finally," he says. Looks up at the sky.
"Every sunset here feels like the first one
I've ever seen. It's so . . ."

"I know. Perfect."

He wins the last round and gets to play for a prize
and when he wins a stuffed bear as big as my bed,
he carries it on his back and we ride off into the sunset.

Beach Cleanup

"Who needs gloves?" Mia asks,
standing at the entrance to Centre Street Beach.
She is welcoming everyone,
making sure folks know why we are here.

It is Take Back Our Island Day
and there are dozens of locals, volunteers, and tourists
all gathered together to shape up the shoreline.

"Thank you for coming out today!" Zach shouts
so that everyone can hear. We stand close around.
"This is our day. We will travel up to Holgate
and down toward Ship Bottom, picking up trash
and anything left behind. We want to make it
even more beautiful. That means stay off the dunes,
but look closely at all other parts of the beaches.
Pay attention. Don't leave anything behind.
We are here to love and honor this island.
Am I right?"

Everyone cheers and calls out *yes* and *thank you*.

Mia, Isa, and I make sure everyone has bags
and protective gear if they need it. We explain
the layout and where we'll be walking.
Tell any newcomers about who we are
and what we're about.

"It's a beautiful day to make this beach SPOTLESS,"
Mia calls out. "Follow our lead. Meet back here
in four hours to celebrate all our hard work."

Milo Shows Up

Just before we head out in teams.
Zach, Mia, and Isa wave him over.
I smile bigger than I expect when I see him.

"So, Eliza's got you cleaning up the place, huh?
I just don't know if that's the way to sell the island,"
Zach says, elbowing me and smiling.
"Picking up trash, combing through the beaches . . ."

"Uh . . . it's exactly how you love something.
You take care of it. You make it look good.
You honor it. You . . ."

"You knew we needed more hands," Isa says,
and I nod in her direction. Everyone laughs
and I can't help but want to share more with Milo,
even if I still have my guard up.

"Well, we need you," I say, handing Milo a bag.
"You can walk with me, be on my team."

"I already am," Milo says,
and I do not have to look up
to know that all of their eyes
are on me.

How do you love something

that could disappear?

How do you fall for someone
who will leave? Who was never meant
to stay in the first place?

How can you convince someone
to love the place you carry with you
always?

How can you hang on to a dream?
Hang on to a barrier island
with only one entrance
and one exit? I want to leave
and want to stay put
all at once.

Want him to see all of it
know all of me. See the island
and me for all our complications.

The Mistake

"Eliza, Ada, Jack! Could you three
get down here?" my dad calls up.
"Why do I always need to shout
in a house that's this small?"

He is standing at the doorway
headed out to work. All of us
stay huddled in the stairway.

"Dad, it's seven thirty a.m. And summer.
Why are you yelling?" Ada asks,
rubbing her eyes and leaning on me.

"Something's been bothering me
and I thought you kids might help.
But since you've been out every night,"
he says, eyeing me now,
"I haven't been able to check in,
so figured I'd ask this morning."

We all stare—not having a clue
what he's talking about.

"Dad—ask already. I can still sleep
for another half hour before work.
Come on!" I say, annoyed now.

"Any of you hear about a group
vandalizing some of the new houses?"

As soon as he says it, my heart stops.
Hope he can't read my face.

"Not that I know of," Ada says.
"No one I know would be that stupid.
Everyone knows everything
on this little island."

I resist the urge to kick her.

"Well, I don't know what's going on.
But we've seen the same signs
in a couple of houses
down by the reserve.
And I figured you all
are always hanging out down there.
Thought you might've seen something,"
he finishes.

"Uh, let's be clear. Eliza's the only one
who spends time partying down there
since I have spent most of the summer
babysitting *this one*," Ada says,
putting her arm around Jack.

"Shut up! You're not my babysitter,"
Jack says.

"*You* shut up. Yes, I am!"

"Enough! You two. Back to bed,"
my dad says, and they try to race each other
back up the stairs.

So then it's just me and dad—staring at each other.
Part of me thinks he might know more

than he's letting on. I stay quiet.
In hopes that I'm wrong.

"Could you just keep an ear out for me?
I'm thinking it might be some of these new kids.
Can't imagine any of your friends would do something
like that. Something so disrespectful. Anyway,
let me know if you hear anything?
Or if any of your buddies hear? Keep us posted.
We're delayed on it because the team
wants to know who's behind this.
They don't wanna have to go over it
all over again. So, help your old dad out, huh?"

"Yeah, yeah—of course. For sure," I lie
and hope he can't see my face
in the early-morning light.

Try and keep a low profile. Hope it goes away.
Hope they forget and move on. Try and move on
myself. Ashamed it was my idea in the first place.

Friday, July 29 | Climate Justice Seekers Meet-Up
　　Five weeks to demolition . . .

I don't tell Milo about our next climate meeting
and go myself to meet up with everyone.
We start in a circle talking about fundraising,
sharing all of our small group updates
and moving on to community events to support the island.

There is another guest tonight—Gloria Hernandez,
a climate activist from the city who works
with UPROSE, Brooklyn's oldest Latino community-based
organization. Isa and her mom set it all up.
The speaker is a friend of the Diaz family.
As one of the biggest organizers for young people of color
rising up against climate change,
she is holding nothing back.
She is holding all of us accountable.

Gloria Says

"Small actions can make a big difference."
She is looking directly at us.
"What are you here to fight for?
You are not in this alone.
Each island is in this together. Always.
Flash floods, mudslides, roofs torn
clear off houses. You have to look
at the global conditions. It is here on LBI,
but it is also everywhere.
Don't forget that."

She keeps on asking us:
Who is the most affected by climate change?
Do not leave those people out.
Call them in.
Do the work you need to do.
Fight back.
Bring everyone along with you.
Look closer. Keep pealing back the layers.

Isa stands up now, reminds the group of this:
"We have to pay attention. See who is the most hurt.
It is the Indigenous communities
in Nicaragua and Honduras.
It is those struggling in Puerto Rico.
It was Black communities during Hurricane Katrina
when the levees broke and people were left
on their rooftops waving flags, with no help in sight.
Who gets hit the hardest? Bangladesh, Manila, Cartagena.
All the places that flood, are flooded.

Not enough help and not enough global action.
We cannot forget."

"Think of that every time you plan an event
or a protest or a sit-in. Every time you think
of what to do. Keep that in your mind,"
Gloria tells us. She is helping
as we plan the clambake and all our fundraisers.
She ends by sharing this quote:

"The people least responsible for climate change
are among the most hurt by its consequences."
Somini Sengupta and Julfikar Ali Manik, *New York Times*

At night in bed

When sleep feels distant
far away—absent to me,
I say the names
of all the hurricanes
and tropical storms
that stay stuck—rooted
in my mind and keep me
from closing my eyes.
Every time I do, I see them
and then say them out loud
like a reverse prayer.
Untangle them in my mind.
Sandy, Maria, Paloma, Ingrid,
Camille, Fay, Rita, Wilma, Paulette.
I know they began using men's names
in the '70s, but from the '50s
until 1979, they were all named
after women. And I can't help
but see them in my mind.
Alicia, Diana, Opal, Roxanne,
Joan, Irene, Claudette, Idalia,
try and look them in the eye
see what they carry with them
and what they will leave behind.
Try and undo the damage.
Unimagine the traumas.
Plead with them,
try and calm
the surge and storm
in them.
Beg them to take charge

the way all the women I know
and love have done—*are doing*
to mend all the breaking.
Urge them to unwind,
swallow back the sea,
let the waters recede,
go back to the ocean
where they belong.

Been thinking of home

Can't stop my mind from running
then sinking, then drowning.
It's always the same. Float, then flail,
sink, then disappear. My dreams—drenched.

Home is an island
& then becomes a raft
& then it's just me
descending.

Because that's the way the ocean moves.
It has not one care about bodies or objects
no concern for homes or shops,
only washing everything—away.

& let me be clear, I love it with all of me.
Love its salt & wave. Love its murky & dangerous.
Love its sand & tide. Love its seashell & plankton.
Love the way it holds me. Floats me. Washes me.

But this anger is something new. Unexpected.
All I see. Is everything. Disappearing.
Right in front of me. A flood of loss
All of me, plunging
below.

In Therapy

I realize that there are parts of me
I am keeping hidden from Milo
and my family too.

My anxiety and anger. Our meetings.
Therapy. I don't tell Milo about that either.
Just say I have something to do after work
and will meet up with him later. Lie.

Some things should be kept close to yourself
and this feels like one of them. Don't share
too much. Not about the sleeplessness
or any of the irrational fears that creep in.

Monica—My Therapist:
Eliza—how are you? You look well. You look
like you are taking care of yourself. Sleeping?
Tell me. What is on your mind these days.

Me:
Spill it. Tell about Milo—and what feels like
my whole life story. Say I think I am falling
for someone who might not be right for me.
And what's the point of falling in love anyway
if the world is going to go ahead and end?
Say my mind is still caught up in floods
and damage. Melting glaciers and mudslides,
fires in California and Australia. Jakarta
is still sinking under the Java Sea. Seawalls
and freakish storm surges. Unsafe drinking
water. Overflooded canals. Everywhere

I look I see homes crumbling. Say look
I am trying my best. And Milo is making
it better. But still, thoughts creep in
and make a home in my head. My mind
crammed up inside.

Monica—My Therapist:
Tells me to do more deep breathing.
Slow it way down. Be in the moment.
Don't keep trying to imagine the future. Be
still. Be here. Be now. Present. Accounted for.
Plant your feet. You are here. Right now.
Breathe in. Breathe out. Stay present. Stay calm.
Start again.

Me:
I like someone. His name is Milo Harris.
I've spent the whole week with him.
Showing him the island. Everything I love.
I guess it's dating. But we haven't kissed yet—
not that it's a big deal. But we haven't.
And I didn't invite him to the climate meeting
because I don't even know if I trust him yet
and I definitely didn't tell him I stayed up late
researching shrinking glaciers in the Himalayas
or how red meat and dairy production accounts
for nearly 15 percent of all global carbon emissions
because if he knew that was on my mind,
he might . . .

Monica—My Therapist:
Breathe. Calming breaths. Pause. Slow down.

Me:
I am scared of the future. And worried
that if we don't do something about the climate
we won't even have a future to be worried about.
And telling him might scare him away.
But I don't even know exactly how I feel.
So I guess I need to figure that out myself.

I do my best

to stay in the moment.
I stay in it when Milo
meets me on the beach
sits beside me
on the bench
high near the dunes
And leans into me.
Stay in it
while we surf
catch waves
and ride.
Stay in it
while cruising
up the boulevard
for fried clams
and rounds
of raw oysters.
Stay in it
when he follows
me home
for a few
extra minutes
of riding
beside
me.

"I Want to Know More"

"I've never met anyone like you," Milo says,
standing in our yard.
The rocks surround his bare feet.
His smile feels permanent—lasting and lasting.
Reaches me.

"What do you mean?" I ask.
Wanting to know more.

I keep on. Breathing. Breaths in and out.
The way I have practiced. The way
I know how.

"I mean, you shake me.
I feel all turned around when you're with me.
Like I can't catch my breath
or I feel dizzy or lost.
Like when the waves take me down."

"They do that a lot," I say.

He starts to laugh. "Yeah, I have A LOT
of experience getting knocked out by waves.
But you know how you tell me to just be,
just wait it out? Let the ocean take me
wherever it needs to. Surrender.
And when I do, I get all lost
in my head. I feel weightless.
Loose. That's how I feel when I'm with you.
You can take me anywhere. I trust you.
Believe what you say. You're so

sure of yourself. Of this island.
It's like you know some secret
to feeling at home
in your body
in your town
in this place.
You know who you are.
And that makes me want to know
everything I possibly can."

My skin tingles

feels the heat coming from him.
He doesn't stop, keeps talking,
telling me things I had forgotten
about myself.
I am remembering
who I used to be.
Before the storm.

"I feel like I know the whole island now.
I know the best places to hang, to eat,
the best waves to catch. Best water slides.
I definitely know how to keep up with you
on a bike—that took some work.
And I love watching you in the water.
It's like you know exactly
where you want and need to be.
And I want to be part of that.
I wanna know more.
I wanna know everything
all there is to know about you now.
What you want and dream about.
Everything.
Can I know everything?" he asks, stepping closer.
"And can you keep teaching me how to surf?
I mean just because I know the best places
to catch a wave, doesn't mean
I actually know how to catch them yet.
Since I'm pretty terrible at it still.
I need you."

And when he says that,
I can't help it. I reach up,
hold the back of his neck
in the palm of my hand
and press my lips to his.
A first kiss
because I can't be patient anymore.
Want him too much.
Can't wait any longer.
So there we stand.
Clear in front of my house.
My mouth open to his.
Reaching.
Holding on.

And then the kissing lasts forever

Or that's what it feels like. His mouth on mine
and then my neck and shoulders. A heat rising, rising.

I feel dizzy with want. As if we waited too long
and are both beneath the waves together.
Knocked loose by each other.

There is a hunger from him I did not know existed
or was this strong. He holds my face in his palms.

"You are the ocean to me," he says.

I shake my head. "Is that a line you say to every girl?"

"Uhh . . . no! I have never compared anyone else
to a massive body of water that could take me under."

"You think I could take you under?"

"I think you already have."

I Need to See You Again

"Hey, this weekend, I was wondering
if I can plan the date . . . I mean just the day."

"The date? Did you call it a date? Is this . . .
are we going on dates?" I ask, confused
but wanting him to say yes.

"Oh . . . I thought . . . uh . . . it kind of feels like
we are, so . . . yeah. If that's what you want.
Because that's what I want. Look,
I can't stop thinking about you.
I go to sleep thinking about you,
I wake up from dreams of you,
I am gonna be thinking about you
and your lips and this kiss."
He kisses me again
and I think we will never stop
kissing on the dock
after the sun is down
and everyone has left to go home.
I never want my lips away from his.
and I am starting to understand
what he meant by being caught
in a wave of this feeling.

"What I am saying," he says,
interrupting my mind and its wander.
"What I am trying to make clear to you,
is that I want to spend every single day
that I am here with you. I don't wanna
ever be away from you.

That's exactly how I'm feeling.
If you want to know the truth.
So yeah. Can I plan the next date?"

"Definitely," I say, coming up for air.

Later

I find myself
falling asleep
without naming hurricanes
or tropical storms at all.
Fall asleep counting
the times
our lips touched
outside
and the beats
of my heart
and the chills
I get
every time
I think
of Milo.
So I stay
counting
the days
and hours
and seconds
I have
to spend
with him
instead.

Friday, August 5 | Climate Justice Seekers Meet-Up
Four weeks to demolition . . .

"Okay, okay. Let's look at the big picture here.
We have more to do and we can't talk
about you and Milo and your love affair
all afternoon. Especially when all you two
have done is kiss. It's a little boring still.
So we have to move on," Zach says,
and we all laugh, but also agree.
We have work to do.

"Four weeks is no time at all!
But we are so far ahead.
We have so many people
who have RSVP'd.
We are moving.
And our messaging is clear!"
Isa adds. Proud of herself.

"Remember we are the ones
that will make this change happen.
It's all up to us," Isa reminds us,
echoing what Gloria said
at our last meeting.
"This is a climate emergency.
We are in a state of crisis.
So we need to show up
for this challenge. This
is on us."

We brainstorm ideas and visions.
What is a climate emergency?
Who is shaped by it?
Who needs to know?

"The clambake is pretty much planned,"
Zach reminds us. "Next up
is figuring out what our sit-in looks like.
And are we really prepared to protect
Clam Cove Reserve?"

All Our Energy

All our

hustle

reactions

responses

movements

plans

power

and motions.

All of it

is in service

to the marshlands

now.

On Saturday night

I get ready for real. Because suddenly,
it really does feel different.
Since the week we spent together,
since therapy, since the first kiss,
since I remembered to breathe.

He knocks on the door and I answer with my family
somehow all standing behind me. They want to know
who I have been spending all of my extra time with.

Mom and Dad shake his hand. Ada leans in the doorway
judging him and us. And Jack nods his head in Milo's direction.
All of us huddled together in the doorway.

"Everyone, this is Milo . . . and also super awkward.
Could you all go back inside and do whatever
else it was you were doing. Please?"

My mom offers cold drinks. My dad offers advice
for the best meals besides Crabs 'n' Cakes
and Ada asks him where he's taking me.
Somehow I get out from under
all the attention and close the door.

"I am soooo sorry for my family," I say,
looking around for his ride. I am expecting
the Escalade, so when we close the door
and I see that he has parked the same beat-up
old hand-me-down bike from Ada
that he borrowed a week ago,
I start to laugh.

"What? You didn't think we were gonna drive?
Don't you care about the environment?
We don't need pollutants, toxic hydrocarbons.
Even I know that. Who needs a car?"

So we ride

Keep our bikes going and going.
He tells me he's planned the perfect way
to spend the night.

"Just follow me," he calls behind him.
He takes the lead, heading north
on the boulevard, our hair flying
in the night breeze. We drive down
past the Clam Cove Reserve and the old motels
that dot the end of the island, the tiny
houses that lead to the mansions.
And suddenly, we get close to the end.
I can see the monster house we tagged
just weeks ago. Still in construction,
still reminding me of the damage—
what we did and what they're doing
by building right up on the water's edge.

"Where are we going?" I call ahead.
"That beach is closed off. No one
is allowed there," I say, stopping my bike.

He pauses too. Looks at me. "Come on.
We're not going to the beach.
I packed a picnic. We're going to my house,"
he says, and right then, he points to it—
the same place where we spray-painted
the waves and all those words, the ones
I have been lying to my dad about,
the ones I have been lying to myself about,

the ones I have been trying to forget.
We park our bikes and I start to sweat.

He smiles. "Are you surprised?
This is our new house. Of course
it still has a lot of work
and there were some issues
with some vandalism
a while back, but I think it's all good now,
so we can go inside and check it out.
I was just waiting
for tonight
for the perfect time
to show you how close.
I mean—we're practically neighbors."

I swallow hard

My heart wailing
inside my chest.
Panic setting in.

"Wow. That's amazing. Um . . .
that's so cool. But, uh . . . looks like
too much construction is still happening.
I don't wanna interrupt . . . ya know,
we could just sit on the beach."

"No, come on. I wanna show you," he says,
and pulls me along.

We walk into the house and I start
to flash back again. To the beginning
of summer. Just weeks ago.
He is excited, nervous,
as he leads me up the stairs.
Starts to tell me about each room
the decks that open up
on each floor.
I am flooded with feelings
my nerves overtaking me.
I start to think that maybe
he's right and it's all covered up
since most of the work
has been done on the first floor,
but as soon as we get to the second,
I see our waves, all the colors looping
together. Milo looks around and I know
he's seeing it for the first time,

our words and the statements we made.
So sure of ourselves.
So cocky and more than a little obnoxious.
There they are in all those colors.
Metallic Gold. Satin Aqua. Gloss Berry.
All of it coming back to me.

Go home

Stop
Destroyer
Stop destroying our island
You're not welcome here

Written on all the makeshift walls
and across beams. Milo stands in front.
"Wow," he says. "I'm sorry . . . I didn't . . .
I didn't realize it was this bad.
My dad mentioned it, but . . ." He looks at me.
"Who would do this?"

I shake my head. "Milo, I'm sure
it was just kids. This is . . . no big deal."

He looks at me and then climbs
to the third floor. I stay below
and try to stop him, know
what's coming next.

"Milo, wait!"

"'Wave Whisperer,'" he shouts down
to me. To my embarrassment.
And shame too. "What the hell, Eliza?
What is this? Did you and your friends
do this? How did you even know
it was my house? Why?
Why would you do this?"

I run up the stairs. "I'm so sorry.
We had no idea this was your house."

"Why would you do it to anyone's house?"

"We didn't. We were drunk. That's no excuse.
It was stupid. I'm sorry," I say again.
"It's just . . . it was just about this house—
uh . . . mansion. I don't know . . . we saw it
taking up so much space and I don't know . . .
wanted it to disappear. Or wanted whoever it was
building it to know that . . ."

"We're not welcome. I get it. Guess you've been
trying to tell me that in some way—all summer.
These last few weeks
you've been getting me to love it here,
feel like I belong. When all the time
you don't even really want me here."

"Milo," I call out,
but he's already down the stairs
then another flight
and out the door
before I can even say goodbye.

Shame

The ride home on the boulevard
is lonely. Ashamed of myself
that I didn't know better
that I wasn't thinking
of anyone else.

As soon as I get to our yard,
Ada and Jack are in the hammock
both of them swinging
back and forth and reading.
They look at me.
Ada cranes her neck
to see where Milo is hiding.

"Why are you home?" she asks.
"Thought this was your big night.
Milo making the plans—the whole
date night. What happened?"

I lean my bike in the rocks
and sit at the picnic table.

"I'm an idiot," I say,
look at both of them
try to decide what to admit
and what to leave out,
but I have to tell someone
get it off my heart.

"What'd you do?" Jack asks,
both of them looking right at me.
And I know I have to tell someone.

"It was so dumb. A few weeks ago
after the party on Rosemma,
we had all this extra spray paint,
and we were a little drunk
and we were the ones
that tagged up a couple of those
big houses on the beach.
The one massive house
at the end of the island
and a couple of others too."

"What?" Jack asks, leaning in
listening close now to the story.
"You trashed a house?"

"No, no, we didn't trash it
we just marked it up a little."

Proof

"So that was you?" my father asks,
and I whip around to see him walking
from the shed. Kicking sand
from his work boots.
Listening in the whole time.

"Dad! I didn't . . . I didn't even know
you were back there," I say, glaring at Ada.

She shrugs her shoulders, mouths *Sorry*,
whispers, "We didn't know
what you were gonna say."

"That was you? You and your friends
who did that? Who defaced that property?
And you said nothing to me when I asked?
Acting like you were gonna find out for me?
You knew we were waiting to work on it
trying to see if we could find out who did it.
And I come to find it was my own daughter?"
he says, starting to raise his voice now.
"That's a house I worked on. That my crew
worked on. My sweat is in that house.
And you and your friends tagged it up
like it was nothing. Like the work I did was nothing,"
he finishes, looking dead at me.

"I know. I'm so sorry. We didn't think . . ."

"That's right. You didn't think.
Eliza, sometimes you are so caught up

in doing what's right for the planet
and doing what's right for the island
and fighting for climate change
that you don't see clearly. You're lost.
Don't see what's right in front of you.
It's selfish. And childish," he says,
running his hands through his hair.

"Wait, hold up. What does this
have to do with Milo? And your date?"
Ada asks, steering us back to the point.

"It's his house!" I shout, trying my hardest
not to cry. Knowing my dad is right
but mad at him at the same time.
"His family is building it.
The same family
that made fun of our boat
and the same one that's building
a million-dollar house
on prime beachfront real estate.
And you are just helping his family
make this island less affordable
for people like us. People who love
it here. People who want this place
to survive."

"Work is work, Eliza. You know that.
And there is no shame in what I do.
But there is in vandalizing and destroying
someone's property because they don't see
the world the exact same way you do.
It's time for you to grow up. And you

better believe that you and your friends
will be paying for any of the damages."
He shakes his head while walking away.
"And you're grounded too," he adds.

"Where would I even want to go?"
I shout, beating him inside
and trying to get a second
of quiet. A minute to myself.

Disaster

great damage
disruption
catastrophe.

Disaster-ologist—
It's a thing. Something
I think I could do.
The study of disasters.
Watch them take shape.
Figure out
how to stop them
in their tracks.

Disaster-ology
the study of
the act of destroying
every good thing
in your path.

Apologies

The next morning, my friends
all come to me. All of them
pissed that my dad knows
and pissed that their folks
know too.

He called everyone's house.
And gave us a lecture
over fried eggs
and hashbrowns.

Said we could meet
on the picnic tables
outside, but my week
would look like work
and then home. Home
and then work.

"Your dad is harsh,"
Zach says, kicking back
in the hammock.

"He's not playing," I say,
and Isa nods her head.
She's grounded too.
Out families—the same.

"My dad's pissed,
but he figures taking my pay
is enough of a punishment,"
Mia says, getting settled

on the picnic table.
"At least we can still meet up."

"That's because we have to plan
the clambake. Which helps
the island. Which helps
the shack and our families
and . . . I can't even believe
he's that mad."

"Your dad or Milo?"
Isa asks.

I catch them up

"It was Milo's house that we tagged up.
'Wave Whisperer.' So stupid," I say.

We unwind the story. Play it back.
Falling. Getting caught. Caught up.

Admit my heart is in it more
than I thought. Catching up with me.

Neon waves and tagged up space
fear of what his family represents

and everything we're working to shape.
We play it all out.

They say:
You have to say you're sorry.
Say it again. Like you mean it.
You can't let this stop you
from falling. You're falling
for him. We can see it.
Own it.

They don't say: Love,
but that is what they mean.

They say:
Swallow all that pride. Be bigger.
Be better. Say more. We've never
seen you like someone like this.

We can see you're falling.
Hard.

I say: This island is home.

They say: Maybe it's big enough
for all of us.

Friday, August 12 | Climate Justice Seekers Meet-Up
    Three weeks to demolition . . .

Climate

Emergency
Atlas
Save me
See me
Emerge
What it means to open up
Cries/crisis
Word play
Enough of
Emerge
See us
Arise
Rise up
We are rising up
Somehow
See us
By the end of the meeting,
we've come up with this—

LBI Clambake for the Climate
        Rise Up with Us
            See the Future

Needs

We need more flyers.
We need stronger hashtags.
We need the best outreach.
We need a few more meetings.
We need clear roles.
We need new jobs.
We need all the organizing.

As for me—
I need to apologize
for my mistake.

In the morning

I lie to my folks
and tell them
we have a meeting
after work.
Ride my bike
all the way
to the LBI Hotel
in the middle
of Ship Bottom.
All shiny
and glitzy
around all edges.
The place
screams new
beach money.
With its indoor
pool and fancy
cabanas. Room
service and everything
with dollar signs.
The front desk
rings his room
but won't tell me
the number. Privacy
and all. I say,
"Tell him it's Eliza.
Eliza Marino."
And cross my fingers
that he'll say
he knows me
and invite me
up.

He comes down instead

Looking like he just woke up,
his hair down around his shoulders
and I've never seen him like this.

We sit in the café near the pool.
The waiter knows him by name.
And when the coffee order comes
he whispers that Zach is a better
barista than anyone in this place.

"I'm glad you're here," he says
before I can even start.

"Look. What we did . . . I just . . .
it wasn't cool. Or funny.
And we didn't know it was you
or your house. Because if we did
we would never have . . ." I stop.
"It doesn't matter. We messed up.
It was my idea. And it was stupid.
And maybe a little immature."

"A little? Yeah. I just have one
question. Why did you do it?
What was the purpose?
Do you all hate the people
who don't live here year-round
so much? What's up with that?"

"No, we don't. I don't! But . . .
maybe a little. It's just that
after the hurricane, people

started coming onto the island
and thinking their money
would make it all better.
So they tore houses down—
our houses. Mia doesn't even live
on the island anymore. She's in Barnegat
because someone bought her house,
tore it down, and turned it into this . . .
into something that doesn't even match
that doesn't even care
about what was there before."

"Destroyed it," Milo says, nodding.
"I get it. I do. And I am sorry
for that too. But I can't change
where I come from,
or who I come from."

"I don't want you to."

"I don't think I believe that.
But I hear you. I do.
I just . . . don't even know
what this is," he says,
pointing at me.
"Or if you even feel
the same way I feel
about you.
Do you?"

And there it is

My heart, feeling like it's hanging
right there outside of my chest,
beating, rocking recklessly.
Knowing I have to tell him
the truth. My truth. All of it.

"Sometimes, I don't know
how to feel about this island
or the people who only spend
part of the time here. Just part
of their lives. When we're all here
always. Forever. Every day
of the year. So we deal with
the empty, quiet winters
and the erosion
and the disappearing shorelines
and the endless flooding
and the stupid articles
in the *New York Times*
that say: the Jersey Shore
is over. We deal with that.
And the people
who summer here,
who vacation here,
take all our resources
and all our goodness
and get all the tax breaks
and all the sunshine
and all the good waves
but they don't have to deal
with anything once they drive

over the bridge
and off this island.
I love this place forever.
And I want everyone
who visits or spends time
to love it too."

Then I pause . . . take a breath

know there is more
that needs to be said
and so I do.

"But at the same time
I really like you too.
Like really, really
can't go to sleep at night
because I'm thinking of you
like you, too.
And I want you to stay
or be here as long as you can.
Because being out in the ocean
with you feels endless.
It makes me feel alive
and like I want to do everything
I possibly can
so that we can stay there
together
for as long as possible.
I want to kiss you
forever.
And I've never said that
to anyone.
I've never felt that
with anyone.
And I can't stand
not being with you
or beside you
or feeling you next to me.
And I want you to stay.

I want you to fight with us
for this place
for this home."

I pause. Take another breath.
Know I need to keep breathing
in order to keep kissing
and I so want to keep kissing.

"And I want to do this,"
and I lean across the table
and put my mouth on his.
And want to keep it there
infinitely.

"Well look who it is!"

I hear a voice right near me, over me.

"Oh, hey. Olive," Milo says, pulling
away from me and looking above my head.

I turn around. His stepmom. Hovering.
Standing so close, I can smell her perfume.
"Why in the world are you two sitting here
when you could be in our apartment?" she asks.

I look at Milo, who has his head bent down.

"I remember you. From the boatyard, right?
What was your name again?"
She is talking so fast I can hardly keep up.

"Come on up. Offer her a snack, a drink.
Don't be rude," she scolds Milo.
"I insist."

And I find myself gathering my bag and following.
Wanting to know as much about Milo
as possible.

We ride the elevator

to the penthouse. It opens up
to the apartment—the hotel in the sky.
My jaw is on the ground. For real.

We walk into the living room
and Olive clicks on the lights and sound
and suddenly music is coming from all speakers.

Milo has his head tilted up—not looking at me.
"Don't be scared. Come on in, you two.
Don't be rude. Milo, go ahead. Show Eliza around."

So he does, leading me from room to room.
Cannot believe my eyes. Or the fact that I had no idea
that a place like this even existed on the island at all.
I feel both excited and numb.
Want to stay in Milo's room
and make out all day.
And also rage against all this excess.
And all this privilege and all these kitchen appliances.
I am struck by it all. My breath really gone now
as Olive pulls food out and talks about
how the island is changing. Better. Bigger. More.

Olive says

"I grew up coming here summers from Philly
and we just loved it. But you know . . . it was always
a little rough around the edges. But now!
It's almost like the Hamptons. But better. More edge,"
she says, winking at me. "You all summer here?"

"No. Eliza lives here year-round," Milo answers.

"A true local! I love it. You must have lots of stories.
I bet it gets so lonely here in the winter."
She smiles at me. Milo sighs.
I can tell he wants her to disappear
and now I know why he didn't invite me up in the first place.

"There used to be a joke—it's sort of inappropriate . . ."

"Then don't tell it," Milo says.

"No, but it's funny! They used to say
that the only people who lived on the island
year round . . ."

"Were drunks and sluts, right?" I finish.
I've heard this one too many times.

She starts to giggle. "Yes! That's it. Because
the only things to do are drink and . . ."

"Olive . . . can you stop saying everything
that comes to your mind?" Milo asks,
standing up, pushing the table back.

So we all stand there.
Silent.
Trying to figure out
what comes next.

The definition of risk

is exposure to danger.

Being exposed to Milo
and his family and their money
and their relationship to this island
and how they treat it and how they see it
would be considered a risk.

I am willing to take.

So I invite him
to our next
climate meeting.

Friday, August 19 | Climate Justice Seekers Meet-Up
Two weeks to demolition . . .

"If we don't protect the land, who will?"
Isa says, starting the meeting. Everyone
agrees. She has the most powerful
voice. I stand beside her. This bond
unbreakable. We welcome the new folks,
ask people to stand up and say how and why
they are here with us.

"Remember, this island is the only place
that we think of as our home,
the only place we've ever known,
the only spot that holds our history,
who we were before. And who we are
now. There will be no new homes
to take the place of where we come from,"
I add, glancing at Milo. Nervous,
but glad he is here with us. Want him to see
all of who we are and what we're fighting for.

Milo introduces himself and says hello.
"I know all these awesome people.
I moved to the island with my family
and want to protect this place too. Think
of it as home now."

The Big Picture

He sits with us in our working groups.
We are in charge of last-minute promotions
and getting everyone at the clambake.
Spreading the word far and wide.
Milo can help. He has experience
with social media campaigns
and getting people engaged.

"So I just want to get clear
about what the big push is all about.
Is it just against development? Or more?
I know we wanna fight global warming,
and over construction on the island,
but what's the main message for this event?"

They all stop and look at Milo. Realizing
I've kept him way out of the loop
and haven't even mentioned
Clam Cove Reserve.
All this time spent with him
and no mention
of what is closest to my heart.

"Eliza hasn't told you?"

Zach asks, looking right at me.
And then Isa and Mia are staring too
with questions in their eyes.

"Well, first of all, since the hurricane,
this island is struggling to hold on to land
and we have been trying to preserve space.
Everyone around us is either building
or rebuilding from the storm.
It's an endless cycle
and the shoreline is disappearing.
Erosion, crowded beaches,
the Army Corps of Engineers
just pumping in more sand
to build up dunes again.
And at the same time
all these new, luxury buildings
are taking up land.
Land we grew up on,
land our families
have helped protect."

Milo is listening.
Nodding along.
And it makes me want to tell him everything.

"Everyone who shows up here
thinks they can just take over.
Not ask us what we want
or what matters to us," Isa adds.
"So we've been working together

all these weeks to protect the marshlands.
It's called Clam Cove Reserve.
There's this big developer
trying to come in and take away
some of the only remaining marshlands
on the whole island. We're trying
to raise awareness—get the word out."

"We're trying to stop it, basically," I say.
Milo has a faraway look on his face,
but when I ask him what's wrong,
he just smiles and reaches for my hand
under the table. Holds on to it.

"First of all, you have to want it"

"I want it," he says, looking right at me.

"Not me," I say, trying to pretend shock.
"The wave. Focus. You need to want the ride.
The freedom. You gotta watch for it.
Wait for it. This is called patience.
This is the calm before."

Surfing starts up again since I'm not grounded
anymore. And every day, I wake thinking
about Milo. About being in his arms, about
his questions, about being alone—out on the sea.

It is six a.m. and the sun is still hidden. It's just us
and a few other early risers floating on their boards.
This is always my favorite time of day. Quiet, serene.
Everything feels possible out here. Only the sound
of waves hitting the shoreline. Only the two of us
coasting—all weightless, all loose. He is better now.
Can balance on the board. Pulls up and we both sit,
our legs straddling and the water pushing us up and down.

"Can I ask you a question?" I say, suddenly brave
out on these waves.

"Anything," he answers.

"No, I can't . . . never mind. It's weird."

"Okay, now I have to know. Just ask."

"Fine, but I promise it's intense." I look out
into the blue sky.

"You're intense. I like that about you. Now ask."

"How do you want to be remembered when you die?"

"Wow," he says. "I was so not expecting that."
I laugh but say nothing. Just wait for his answer.

"I want people to know I was my own person.
That I didn't rely on my family or their connections
or their money. That I stood up on my own."

Ever since the hurricane

The same questions stay on our minds.

Who do we want to be?
How will we be remembered?

That part is essential. We want to be remembered
for what we believed in,
for what we risked
for what we took action on.

Let us be known as the kids who never stopped.
Unrelenting. Never. No stopping.
Celebrating the ocean and every changing tide.
Honoring the salt and every memory
connected to the sea. Let us tell its story
to all. Let us be a part of the telling.

What water can do

The kind of damage.
I have been thinking
of what is lost at sea.
What can drown
and never come up for air.
This new love
makes me feel like
I am sinking
below.

Crabs 'n' Cakes

Finally, it feels like time to take Milo home.
Not to my house, but to the restaurant,
so I ask my mom and Yara if they will stay open late
and make a big meal for all of us. Promise to help.
So I invite Milo and the whole crew over.
Ada, Jack, Mateo, Rio, and Marisol come.
It is a night for families, so my dad and Mr. Diaz
show up too. All of us in the kitchen and spreading
out across the small tabletops.

Yara and Nina's is a shrine to women and family.
The whole place wallpapered in history, all
their ancestors showing up in photographs
and the endless stories they tell. To us.
To each other, to their endless stream
of customers. The shack is mostly breakfast
and lunch and late-afternoon snacks, so this
is special. And only happens a few times
each summer. When Yara and Nina show out
with their kitchen skills. They are doing this
as much for me as for the clambake.
Trying out new recipes for the party.
Since they are family.
Since they are the best of the best.
Since they represent us and this island.

I introduce everyone to Milo.
He puts an apron on
and slices shallots and garlic with my mom.
My dad gives me a nudge and wink to show he approves
of this, of us. We play loud pop music and salsa,

R & B and oldies that the adults sing loud to.
We dance our faces off.
And then we devour the dinner.
The clam chowder. Softshell crabs seasoned perfectly.
Clams on the half shell and Jersey scallops
drowning in butter. Shrimp scampi.
Mom and Yara show off. I love it.
Love that Milo can see how much
and how hard we all love.

People say Jersey Strong

and when I'm here with these people,
I know they mean us.

"We can be our own leaders.
It's not just one of us
it's all, all of us.
The whole island like a wave
rising. We are high tide itself.
We rise and rest as one,"
my mom says.
All of us sitting at the tables listening.

Zach starts to make espresso
and Isa scoops up ice cream.
Sugar high.

Yara says, "You have to write it down.
Call it to you.
Intentions are everything.
What do you want in your life?"

We take their advice.
Try to build our own ideas and visions
for now and the future.
How to sustain.
Maintain.
Just be.

Some nights

even after
gathering
and loving
so many
my mind
gets to racing
and I take my laptop
to the kitchen.
Can't get natural
disasters off my brain
they stay stuck
scrolling through.
So I start my own scroll
to counter it.
Look up storm
after storm.
Hurricanes
Eta and Iota.
Get on social media
to check in
on all my
climate
activists.
Follow their lead.
Lead on my own.
Write it down.
Don't forget
I can do this
we can do this
make change
matter

stop the constant
stop the scroll
be in the now
call what I want
rather than
obsessing
over
what I don't.

Everything feels new all of a sudden

Feels like I could break the cycle.
Could make a change.

My therapist is always saying
to do more mindful breathing.
She calls it a body scan.

So that's what I do.
Close up the laptop.
See the island whole and thriving.
See the marshlands blooming with bay life
and nesting diamondback terrapins.
See them outside my window
with no construction or trucks
or multimillion-dollar deals.
See it complete without all that extra.
Vision what I want
and see it take shape.

So tonight I think about this life—

the one I am trying to love and not
be scared of. I call to me gathering
and space. My community surrounding me
as much as possible. Loving my friends
and family. Making change and creating.
Facing our changing world in a brave
and solid way. I call to me being unafraid.
Working against global warming.
Love, love, love. Creating space
that pushes against and educates and reaches.
Energy that fills me with emotion
and carries weight. Stories that are heavy
but hold me up at the same time.
Traveling all over my mind,
my neighborhood, my island,
the streets of where I live
and eventually the whole world.
Keep feeding my body, my mind.
Reading, sleep, working,
food, sweat, dance, loving, holding.
Yes, I call all of this to me.
Laughing, feasting, resting,
working and love, love, loving.
Let it be true. Soon, soon.

To the lighthouse—

"I need to show you what we're fighting for."

So this time we drive
all the way to Barnegat Light,
the other end of the island
where the walk to the beach
could be a mile
and is the home of the state park
devoted to the lighthouse
where you can climb
the 217 steps and see out
across all of Barnegat Bay and Inlet
to the Atlantic.
172 feet above sea level.

I want to show Milo forever.

And walk him through
the maritime forest
to see black cherry
and sassafras, red cedar
and American holly.
I know all this
because we'd spend
fall weekends here
with other families
walking and playing
fishing and birdwatching
loving the land
and all the stories
of this place.

"Up here, you can see
how much has been
developed and changed
how the island looked
before all the houses
and condos and shops."

I point to the small
patch of forest that we see
way up top.

Milo puts his arms
around my waist,
holds on tight.

"How come you never talk about the hurricane?"

Milo asks. We are sprawled out on a blanket
watching the sun sink slow, slow into the bay.
I've been holding my breath because it's never been
this beautiful. And I've never felt this much.
I don't reply right away, unsure what to say,
how to respond. Don't want to say too much,
but tired of holding on too.

"I talk about it all the time. I mean, I did. Still do.
Mostly to my therapist. Her name's Monica.
I see her every week. She does not go easy on me.
Been seeing her for almost four years," I admit.
He nods.

"Most of the kids I go to school with have been
in therapy at one point or another. I went
when my folks got divorced. It helped.
At least it was someone to talk to—that wasn't them."

I let a breath out. Already feel better.

"Used to be we'd talk about it all the time. Nonstop.
Because all of us went through it. Zach, Isa, Mia—
each of our lives changed because of it. We
got rocked by it. Our families almost went bankrupt,
our house was completely and totally destroyed.
We almost lost my brother," I say—finally,
hearing it out loud bringing all the emotions
right back to me.

"Jack? What?" Milo asks, putting his hand over mine,
and just like that, I am back there—trying to catch
my breath. Trying to hold on. Trying to keep
my brother alive. Breathe in, breathe out.

HOW TO SURVIVE A HURRICANE

FIVE YEARS AGO

Under Water

"Jack, where are you!?
Please, please!
Jack!
Dad!
Help!
I can't find . . . Jack!"

My voice
feels reckless
breaking
shaking
inside me.
I am screaming
yelling for help.
My arms dragging
desperate
through the water
scared I am losing
Jack
and my grip
and my heart
now too
searching
holding
crying.

"Jack!"
"Dad!"

The water
is rushing

pushing
past me
sinking
me
lifting us.

Panic
I reach
for Jack
can't find
him
anywhere.

Searching

Ada is holding tight to the car
the water flooding all around us.

I can see Jack's body rising up
and then getting caught by the surge.

He is small still. The smallest one
of us. Six years old and drowning.

"Mom! Dad!" I scream, my lungs
loud from the street. Lights are off

the houses look empty and lonely. Why
did we stay? I am charging through

the water heavy all over me. I can see
Jack pushing up and trying. Frantic.

My mom and dad come sprinting out
hearing my voice, seeing the downpour

how the tides are heavy on us. They
yell and scream for Jack. His body

appearing and disappearing. Must have
hit his head or hurt himself. He's in pain

calling to us. Screaming right back.
and then—it goes quiet. Slow motion.

My dad sprinting through the salt water
his face a wash of terror and pain.

My mom holds Ada and me close, heaves
beside us. And I do not count the minutes

but seconds. Know from junior lifeguarding
that drowning can go fast. And I hold on.

Blame myself. Blame my parents for sending
us outside. Not knowing the damage.

We should have left. We should have left.
We should have left. We should have left.

One-one thousand
    Two-one thousand
        Three-one thousand

"Where is he?" my mom yells.

My dad is frantic, pushing, searching.
The water blowing and rushing past us.

Hold my breath. Count each second.

Four-one thousand
    Five-one thousand
        Six-one thousand

My dad is flailing, trying over and over to balance,
but loses his grip, each time flipping front to back.

Seven-one thousand
    Eight-one thousand
        Nine-one thousand

My mom is shouting again. Her voice hoarse
and wailing into the night. Mine too. And Ada's.

Ten-one thousand
    Eleven-one thousand
        Twelve-one thousand

"Help!" my dad shouts to no one—crying out.
and suddenly, he reaches down and comes up
holding Jack by the waist. Limp. Dad struggling
to carry him. The water flashing over and up

nearly past his knees now. Moving slow motion
we all push to the house—already starting
to flood now.

"Move, move!" my dad calls.

We race against the water

Rushing in the house now
sprint up the stairs. Attic
is still dry. Dad is gentle,
gentle with Jack's body.
Empty of breath now.
Know Dad can save him
if there is time. If there
is breath inside. "Call 911!"
my dad yells and we do
but we all know the lines
are down. Jack is lying
on the attic floor, lifeless.
His head bleeding, must
have fallen, gotten lost
inside the water, the waves.
My dad listens for breathing,
takes a breath himself.
All his training now.
I am crying huddled beside
Ada who is hyperventilating.
Dad starts chest compressions.
I know this. Lifeguard training.
I know this. Island living.
I know this. Volunteer firefighter.
I know this. Ocean swimming.
100–120 per minute.
Wait for the chest to rise
and then fall again.
Check breath.
Check breath.
Keep on.

Keep on.
Keep on.
Open the airway.
Pinch the nose.
Breathe for him.
My dad hollers
cries out.
Compressions.
Breath.
Breathe for him.
Please.
Please.
Stay
alive.

Jack coughs

sputters water from his nose
and mouth. His body moves.
Comes alive beside us.
My mom calls out.
Her voice carrying beside me.
Hold on to Ada.
Hold on to myself.
All of us a crash of bodies.
Surrounding and struggling
to stay beside each other.
All of us crying and holding.
Holding and crying.
A wash of tears everywhere.
We stay that way
ride out the worst
of the hurricane
as it barrels through
and the ambulance
finally finds us
hours later
still together
still holding on
still
still
alive.

Still catching my own breath

after telling the whole story,
I feel Milo's arms around me.
Holding on to me. To keep me
from drowning too. His mouth
at the base of my shoulder.
"You're safe," he says.
And I believe him. Lean back
and let him hold me. Close.
We stay that way for so long
that the sky starts to lose sun
so we walk to watch it set
over Barnegat Inlet. Just
like fireworks over the water
we stand beside each other
catch the orange glow around
us, all over us. This feeling,
one I never, ever want
to fade.

He makes me feel

Everything.
All at once.
Want and need
coming close together.
The way his skin feels
against mine
is a kind of fire
I have never known.
Lost and trembling.

His skills on the surfboard

and out in the ocean
and right beside me
are getting better too.
So we ride.
Every afternoon
the two of us.
we stay afloat
we do.
ride each flow
grow and grow.

Finally—

Milo catches
his first wave.
We wait
like always
floating
anticipating
watching
taking it in.
I see it first
start to curl
lift up
from the ocean
bed and salt
churning up.
He sees it too.
"Paddle! Go!"
I call to him
want him
want this
for him.
He paddles
hard. His life
depending
riding
free.
Just underneath
he catches it
beneath
the wave
below
and under

riding him
now.
Pushing
him to shore.
He stands up
his arms pumping.
It's only
one minute
but his smile
reaches me
from the beach.
"Yes!" he calls out.
"One hundred percent
pure adrenaline,"
we both say,
yelling
and shouting.
"*Point Break*
was right!
This is
the best
ever,"
he calls out.
And I throw
my arms up
and cheer.

After Surfing

We get back to my house
and no one is home.
Jack and Ada
out on the boat
with Dad.
My mom
still closing up
at the shack.
We stand together
outside.
I look around
and then back to Milo.
And I see my summer.
The one I was hoping
and planning for.
The one in my dreams.
The one that has me here.
Standing in front of a boy
that I am falling all over for.
And I see myself confident.
And ready to take the risks
I keep on talking about.
Jump in.
And something
comes over me.

"Let's take a shower," I say,
and Milo looks at me
then around
the whole block.

"Are you serious?"

"Just to get the sand off.
It's no big deal," I lie,
my heart rushing up
through my chest.

"Uh yes . . . I would love that.
Let's go,"
he answers
following behind,
his palm
on my hip
I guide him.
Our bathing suits
still on,
he asks
if he can
wash my hair.

I say yes.
Because this is more
than I have ever
even wanted.
More
than I can hold on to.

Our outdoor shower is old beach

Old soaps and shampoo bottles
the top open up to the sky.
I watch the clouds pillow
above us. He holds my shoulders
in his palms. Towers over me.
I stand on my tiptoes to reach
his mouth. The taste of spearmint
on his tongue. I am lost. Out
of this shower and what feels like
this world. Worlds away. His
arms feel liquid beside me. He
runs his fingers through my hair
gets the waves tangled in his hands.
Tells me come closer. And so I do.
This tenderness feels unreal. Like
I've left Earth for real now. Orbiting
above. Lost in his touch, in his taste.
Feel him move closer beside me
and just when he does, I hear
car tires over gravel. His eyes widen
and we get tickled—start to laugh
and I put my finger to my lips.

"Go now!" I whisper, my breath
on his neck.

"I love you," he whispers back.
Holds my mouth on his
for a second too long,
and then slips out the door
and onto his bike
cruising away.

Who cares

if my breath
never comes back
to my body.
What do I need
it for now.
Now
that I am lost
for real.

Surprised
and in love
with him
too.

"Will you miss me when I'm gone?" he asks

We are together. Again. This time,
spending the night at Fantasy Island. Alight
with Skee-Ball and games that ping and ring,
he wins me a giant dinosaur that he carries
around with him. Mia and Isa take turns
on the Dragon—riding high into the sky
and Zach and I have our annual battle
of the bumper cars. Everyone cheering
us on. We eat funnel cakes and chocolate-
covered ice cream cones. French fries
dipped in cheese and hot sauce. Sensory
overload for sure. Summer is closing
so tight around us. Heading toward
the end and I am already sad. Yes, yes.
I will miss him when he is gone.

On the Ferris wheel,
he holds me around the waist.

"Oh . . . are you scared?" I ask him,
shifting my weight
so I'm looking him
straight in the eyes.

"Me, never," he says,
but when the ride starts,
he shivers and I slide
closer next to him,
knowing somehow
he needs me beside him.

We stall at the top
and I can feel him tense up.
I want to tell him
that I love him too.

"Come on. You have to look out," I say,
pull him in so he can see everything
the water slides we went down,
the wharf, smell the ocean in the air
see the calm bay. Take it all in.

"From up here, I can almost see
my house. And look! There it is."
I point far in the distance.
"That's the marshland. The one
we're working to save," I say,
touch my hand to his.
He doesn't respond
And when I look at him
he looks pale—scared.

"Are you okay?"

"I have to tell you something"

he says, leans back in his seat.

"Are you afraid of heights?"
I ask, suddenly worried now.
"We shouldn't have come up."

"No, no. I mean, yes, I am definitely
afraid of heights. But that's not it.
It's more than that. It's . . ."
He stops talking and leans over
the edge. Looks where I was pointing.
"It's the marshlands."

"What about it?"

"It's my family. The big developers
you all were talking about.
Hope/Hart Construction.
Olive's last name
and my grandma's last name.
It's us. My dad.
I guess in a way . . . me too."

"What?" I ask, moving away from him
steadying my balance as the passenger car
weaves and loses balance in the sky.

"I know. I'm sorry. I didn't know
how to tell you. When you came over
and we talked, I just . . . I got scared.

Freaked out that you'd leave for good
if you all found out. That everyone
would hate me."

I move away and Milo leans his head
way back. Can't tell if he's catching
tears and trying to push them back in.

"So you lied? So you pretended
that you cared about our island?
Made me believe you wanted to fight?
You liar," I say, moving away from him.

"Look, they're just trying to help. I swear."

"To build up this island. To make it strong.
I get that you're mad. I do,
but I don't want this to change anything.
It doesn't change the way I feel about you."

"It changes everything," I say,
move aside and try to steady my breathing.
Focus on my breath.
In and out.
Slow it down.

The ride rotates around two more times.
I am holding myself now. Rocking
as the ride comes to a stop.

Push my way outside

Exit the park.
Don't bother saying
goodbye or good night.
I'll check in later.
Right now
I need to leave.
Need space.
Recover.
Need to be alone.
Milo rushes to follow.
Says *wait up* and *please*
and *hear me out.*
He follows me
to the docks.
And stands beside me
looking out.

"I'm sorry.
It's not my fault
Can you just wait
and talk to me?"

"How is it not your fault? You knew!
You knew the whole time
and never said anything.
Kept it from me the whole time.
Kept it from all of us."

"I know. And that was messed up.
And I don't even—
what am I supposed to do, Eliza?

Tell me. And I'll do it."

"You think I know?
You think I have any idea
about what to do?
I'm as scared as you.
Scared that we'll lose our home
and everything we've ever known
and worked for.
You. Your family has it all,
but instead of being thankful
you want more. More land and more money
and more of what we've been working so hard
for. All our lives. So the fact that you can't even
think of what to do on your own is just—"

"Pathetic," he says. "I know. But can't you
look at it from their point of view? They love
it here and want other people to visit
and spend time. Development isn't always
bad or wrong. It brings jobs and more money.
And I get your argument about climate change
and I see what you mean about fighting against it,
but we're not the ones you need to be fighting.
Maybe you and your friends are too caught up
in a fight that's not yours. And you can't see
beyond this place," and when he says it
I can see that it's true—he doesn't love it
the same way we do.

And I feel it. In my bones.
Feel that same heaviness.
And loss. He walks me to his car.

I text everyone.
Say I got motion sick on the rides.
Don't say what I am really sick about.

We are silent on the car ride home.
When I say goodbye, I know
I will never see him again.

At home

Mom and Dad sit
laughing and smiling
and cheers-ing
at the kitchen table.
A bottle of wine
open between them.

I try and make it
to my room
but they stop me.

"Come celebrate with us,"
my mom says, pulling out a chair.

"I'm really not in the mood."

"Oh, come on! Ada and Jack
are at the movies. It's just us
in here. Come on. I have chowder,"
she says, since she knows I can't resist.

"What's the big news?"

"Well," my mom starts. "Crabs 'n' Cakes
is getting a second location!"

"What? Where? When? That's amazing!"
Suddenly glad they stopped me,
realizing I needed this good news.

"Down in Harvey Cedars. Right off

Compass Street. Near 80th.
Yara found the space and we looked
today. Beautiful. Lots of foot traffic.
And this summer has been the best
one we've ever had. Thanks to you
and all your friends too. For spreading
the word—sharing who we are, what
we do, what we stand for. I love you,"
my mom says, pulling me in for a hug.
"We have all been through so much
together. This feels like such a reward.
And with the new construction job,"
my mom finishes, looking at Dad now.

"What new construction job?"

I swallow, remembering Milo
and the Hope/Hart project
and don't want to hear anything else
about breaking ground
or what's good for this island
or what I am supposed to feel.

"Go on, tell her. She can handle it,"
Mom says, elbowing him.

"Our team got the bid.
For the new construction.
The Hope/Hart project.
We'll be doing all the inspections,
working close with the team.
We're gonna do all we can
to make it sustainable.
Being that close to it
will help in the long run."

"What?" I say, my eyes clouding over,
feeling I will break or lose my balance,
hearing that name so many times tonight.

"It's a big contract, Eliza.
You know we have to take this."

"But you said yourself that you would never
be a part of that project. You know
it's destroying some of the only marshland
we have left. You know that. Clam Cove Reserve

is for us—for this island. We have to protect
it. Why would you even think of doing this?"
I can hear my voice rising up. Losing breath,
losing balance.

"Eliza, you don't understand everything.
We are just now getting back on our feet.
Five entire years after the hurricane. Just
now. And finally your mom and Yara
have an opportunity to expand
and I can help them make that happen.
We need the money. That is what being
an adult is. Making sacrifices. Sometimes
doing things you don't love."

"You know this is wrong," I say.
"And I understand. Perfectly.
You say you care about the island
and everyone here. About the planet.
But really—when it comes down to it
all you care about are yourselves."

"Enough," my mom says. Eyeing me now.
"That's enough. This is our decision.
And I hope you will be able to see
the bigger picture here. Hope you
can get behind us and our future."

But the truth is

I am not even sure
what the future will look like
if everything we love
is torn apart.

The action is needed
now. The change
can't wait.

& everyone in power
thinks we have forever
to stop it.

Even my own parents
don't believe
in this timeline.

The youngest
are the angriest.

I keep reading that.
I keep feeling that.
The weight
on my chest.

If we don't speak up
who will?

If we don't protest
& shout
& sit in

& rally
will anything happen?
Will anything shift?

I am back in the riptide
& I am sinking.

Always a hurricane . . .

Always a hurricane . . .

Always a hurricane . . .

Stop. My mind running. Maps and oceans
clouding my thoughts. Alone in my room.
How we study the maps and how water moves.
Where does water exist—whose homes
does it threaten to wipe out, to take over
and wash away. Who gets to build up and take over?
How are we supposed to live now?

The way a memory gets lodged, linked
inside of you. The way your whole mind
gets rearranged by the pain. How trauma
stays etched inside of you. Tattoos part of you
and roots in.

My mom says the future and all I see is our past.
The night Jack almost drowned stays lodged
in my head. Can't shake it. My dad running,
my mom screaming. CPR. Breath. Hanging on.
And now—all they want is to cover up the past
what we went through—who we are now.
Aching inside. This is not the summer
I dreamed about. Now, it's the one
I am trying to forget.

The sky is still there—

where it has always been
so I make sure that Jack and Ada
are asleep in the room with me
and then head up to the roof. As witness.
There it is. All blistering and whole
and full of rain. The kind that won't stop,
keeps pouring and flooding
and wrecking everything in its path.
Destructive flow.
And the clouds are not just clouds,
but bodies and stars too,
and it is almost dawn, so the sun
is stretching its way into the day.
Timeless.
I am waiting for an answer.
I am waiting for the right way,
what to do. How to make it all right.
I am waiting for my own breath
like I am waiting for the planet to rotate.
Like I am waiting for Milo to come back
and my dad to change his mind
and my friends to know I am hurting
without me telling them.
I am waiting to be the me I am proud of
and not the one I am scared of being.
I look over toward the sea
full of fish and salt and shells like always.
The universe begins
and begins all over again.

In the morning

Everything feels rough
around the edges.
My eyes are sore
and swollen from crying
and all I want
is more sleep
and to stay in bed
away from it all.
I'm seventeen
and feel like
I'm on the verge
of everything.
That's how
it feels.

Trying so hard
to not be that kid again.
The one so scared of everything.
The one who has been working so hard
to be strong and calm.

But today is all clouds when I wake.
Relieved to see Jack and Ada still asleep,
I walk to the ocean alone.
Unsure of it all.
Afraid I won't make it
and what will be left if I don't.

Ride the waves alone

float
    sunshine
        seashore
            skyline
        erase
    imagine
dunk
    balance
        plank
            stand
        ride
    free

Meditation

On the lifeguard stand,
I stay looking out on the bay.
My whole life flashing
fast forwarding.
The summer
like a dream
I can't wake from.

Breathe in and out.
Count backward.

I know when Isa arrives
because she takes my hand
holds on to it
and reminds me
what we're fighting for.

Monica can tell straight away

that I am lost. Trying to find my way
but struggling to stay above water.

She says: Sit down. Take a breath. Take
it easy. Spill it. She smiles. Tilts her head.

And so I do.

Feel like I am backsliding. So confident
and then so defeated. Falling for someone
who stands for everything I'm against.

She says: Take a step back. Look
at the big picture. Is there anything
you are missing? Can you put yourself
in their place? Can you find a way
to use your voice and hear theirs
at the same time?

I don't answer. Just go quiet again.
Go empty. Get lost again.

The nightmares keep coming—

and lately they won't let up.
Most of the time I'm caught up
waves erasing me somehow
sink and fade.

The water is choppy today

murky—full of big waves
that run and knock me down.

The water gets choppy
starts to push and rush
comes in heavy
against me.

Keep standing and keep
getting pummeled
to the ground.
Try and stand.
Try and fight back
but every time I do
I get kicked to the seabed
each time
sinking
lower
and lower
than
before.

Friday, August 26 | Climate Justice Seekers Meet-Up
One week to demolition . . .

I show up late to the meeting I am supposed to be running.

All eyes are on me.
I know I'm in trouble.
Having forgotten
about too much.

Been trying to surf and swim it all away.
Not paying attention to what needs to get done.

Mia, Isa, and Zach are sitting together
in our working group. They stare at me.

"What? I'm just a few minutes late.
Sorry!" I say. Defensive. I know it.

"And you haven't been returning calls
or texts. Like you're out of it all of a sudden,"
Mia says, looking concerned. I know she is worried,
trying to be gentle with me.

"It's like you're so caught up with Milo that you've
forgotten about what we're trying to do here,"
Zach says. "This was your idea, remember?"

"And all this time you're supposed to be spending
on the clambake and the sit-in
is going to Milo.
I think you're letting what's in *here*
mess with our bigger plans,"

Isa says, pointing her finger
right at my chest.
"This island is your whole heart.
It's everything to you.
Don't just let it go for some guy."

Milo Harris Is Not Just Some Guy

"He's the guy you all convinced me to go for.
A guy you all said I needed to talk to.
To teach, to spend all my time with.
Oh, Eliza! You said it was freedom summer.
Go for it. Live your best life!
Don't be so scared. Take a chance.
That was all of you. And now
now that I'm into him,
now that all I can think about is him,
now that I'm falling in love with him,
it's wrong. I'm wrong.
I'm the one who is letting it all go.
You know what? I can't do this anymore.
If the island is just gonna disappear
then why does it even matter?" I say,
pack up my bag, wave goodbye,
and walk out of the meeting.

I don't tell them that Milo and I
have already said goodbye.
Don't tell them it's already over
between the two of us,
or that I have nowhere to go.

What I Don't Tell Them

is that I'm in love with someone
who is working hard to tear us apart.

That my heart is heavy with loss
and love at the same time. Unmovable.

Breaking for the guy they think
is just some fling. But it's more than that.

And more than this aching feeling
in my chest and head.

I don't tell them about Hope/Hart
or his family name. His history

demolishing our future.
I don't say it out loud.

Because I don't want it
to be true.

Head straight to the dock

Sit alone on the bayside,
watch the water move in
and then out. Dip my toes.
Lean back and look around.
All over there are houses
being built toward the sky,
standing beside the past.
All of us living together.
Look at my house now.
The one we all grew in,
the one we're all out-
growing. It's still home
but now I'm the one
who's ready to leave.
What will it look like
if I walk away?

WHAT IS LEFT
FIVE YEARS AGO

My memory holds everything

The smell of salt everywhere.
Water washing over.
Struggling and holding on.
But watching all the things we love
and care about wash away.
All of it destroyed.
Memories, old photos and stories.
Each item that was saved
and loved and held on to.
We watch it all float away.
Watching your life disappear
is crushing.
I cry so much and so hard
that I am heaving. Sobbing.
Relieved my brother is alive
and breathing again.
But do not know
what we will return to.
Thankful we are safe
and together.
But driving off the island
there is wreckage
everywhere.
Loss and damage
surrounding us.

Our island is under water

and it feels crushing. All of us
safe and out of our home.
Off of our island. Away.
With family now.
Manahawkin is not familiar
or easy. The mainland
is not our home.
I am wrecked.
Every second, can't catch
my breath. Or hope.
Every place we go
people are holding on to tears.
Always on the verge.
At Walmart the woman behind us
breaks right on down.
Weeps with a cart full
of packaged foods,
toilet paper, and toys.
Says, "We lost everything."
And we nod.
My father is always saying,
"We understand."
"What can we do to help?"
He never lets on that we lost everything too.
Or lets it be known that our house was destroyed
and Mom's brand-new restaurant—ruined,
or that we almost lost my brother in the storm.

He does not show emotion. And neither does my mom.
Both of them trying to be too strong for all of us.

So I follow their lead—as long as I can.
Head up, shoulders square.

What do you need? What can we do for you?
Groceries? Supplies? Help with your kids?
Help with rebuilding?
Can we cook you a homemade meal?
We are here for you. What can we do?

And there is always something to do.
Someone to help.

"But what about us? Who will help us?" Ada asks.
I wish I had an answer to that. But I keep on.

We're the ones who make it bad

This is what I know.
I am only twelve,
but can see it is us wrecking
everything in our path.
And I am angry and hurt
and wrecked by it all too.
Everything at the same time.

We're the ones
destroying natural flood protection.
Building right up on the shoreline,
paving roads through the marshland,
ruining all that is natural
all that is in nature.
We wreck.

I am twelve
and already
carrying that with me.
Every day.
Always.

Insurance

only covers
some things
Never everything.
Never all things.
You have to be
prepared.
Wind.
Water.
Flood.
A different one
for every single
type of disaster.
Always prepared
for everything
to go under.
We almost go under
ourselves.
Bankrupt.
Almost belly up
almost lose it all
almost broke for real
is what Dad says.
On the phone
for hours.
My mom crying,
her eyes marked
and wet with tears.
All of us huddled
and scared.
We watch and wait.
See the island

and our family
break down
be drowned
under water.

We hustle

We work
We clean
We remake
We cry
We weep
We laugh
We moan
We ache
We sleep
We swim
We walk
We bleach
We sweep
We empty
We fold
We rinse
We repeat
We rinse
We order
We rush
We push
We press
We bulldoze
We hold
We crush
We crowd
We carry
We cling
We catch
We move
We pack

We sing
We dance
We rally
We hope
We sweat
We pray
We show up again
the next day.

After the hurricane

We thought we'd be alone on the island.
Thought it would return to the locals
& that people would be scared
to buy new properties & new homes.
Thought there would be some relief
from the bigger-is-better problem.
But turns out, just the opposite happened.

Suddenly, twelve months later,
while we were still digging ourselves out of the sinkhole,
people were buying up all of our ruin.
Damaged & destroyed homes were selling,
the market was hotter than ever, or at least
that's what the newspapers kept saying
& everyone was talking about the best summer ever
& saying New Jersey Strong
& while I loved hearing that
& believed every word
I had a hard time watching it in action.

Seeing my mom & Yara hustling every day at the restaurant,
making something out of nothing
& my dad volunteering
to help everyone on the block rebuild.
New Jersey Strong just meant working ourselves
to exhaustion. & when everyone started coming back,
the tourists, the visitors, the weekenders,
it just meant being strong
for everyone else.

New Jersey Strong

It was meant for us, not them.
I didn't want to believe it
for the new people coming in.
The ones who saw our sinking island
and decided they needed a roof deck
for a better view of the waves,
a wading pool,
double outdoor showers,
a hot tub, more apartment complexes
with more grill stations
and more bar tops for mixing more drinks.
They came to remove **FOR SALE** signs
all over our street. Came looking for places
to park their boats, WaveRunners, and paddleboards,
spots to lean their brand-new, shiny surfboards.
Making all the noise and so much racket around us.
Moving in.
Fishing, crabbing, loud construction that cut us off
from hearing the ocean.
Dropped in and expected us to be happy.

New Jersey Strong—expected us to be open arms. Waiting.
New Jersey Strong—*we're here to serve. What can we do for you?*

While our own families struggled to keep afloat.
Everyone else showed up to watch us drown.
And then snatch up what we inevitably
left behind.

But still, they call us New Jersey Strong.

I Want to Claim It

Strength & courage.
Stability & power.
Want to stand up
in my own story.
Share it.
Listen to others
who have been
through it too.

Want to be
unafraid
lasting
even when
my fear
sits so close
beside me.

Being scared
will not fix
the problem.

What does it mean
to face it?
Be a kind of
fearless.
Dare myself
to show up
even
if I am terrified
of the future.

The next morning

the fight feels back.
Not sure what switched
or what changed.
Sleep. The bay.
The moon full
in the sky.
My heart.
Waking.
Accumulation
of breath
and anger
but love too.

Not afraid.
Not soft spoken.
Not backing down.
Not taking no for an answer.
Not scared of what they'll call me.

What I've been through
makes me weathered.
Stronger.
Makes me hustle.
Makes my stamina grow.

I am seventeen
and stronger than before.
Try my best to show up anyway.

Head to the beach to collect shells

The ones that remind me of Isa,
Zach, and Mia. The ones that remind
me of Jack and Ada. My mom and dad.

I want them to know that I am sorry.
That it's possible to be many things
at the same time. To want the fight
and to carry the love all at once.

Gather the smooth and shiny, the rough-
edged ones that peak up from the sand.
Shells with holes from moon snails.
Black and orange bay scallops. Stained
from all the beach replenishing. Buried
from years and years. Gather those too.
Oyster, clam, and scallop shells. All of them.
C-shaped with curves and stretch.
Bring them home. Clean them all together
in the outside shower. Remember Milo
and hold one perfectly curved shell to give.

An offering.

Days Until Demolition

We meet up again.
Know there is more work
and I am ready to jump in.

Zach's posts about the marshlands
and all the photos of the turtles
has caused a reaction on social media.
People on all ends of the island
are fired up. The mainland too.
We have triggered something
inside of them. Seeing their homes,
this way of life being torn apart.

And they're mad as hell too.

The Sit-In

"So wait. Tell me the plan
for after the clambake?
For demolition day
and the marshland protest?
Are we still gonna do it?" I ask,
realizing I've missed the calls
and texts to come up with a solid vision.
Realize I was too much in my own head
to care about what really matters.

"Oh, we planned it.
We're gonna block the site,"
Zach tells me.

"What do you mean?
I thought we were just gonna
spread the word, or . . ."

"It's bigger than that. We're gonna block it.
We're gonna camp out.
We've already been spreading the word.
All over town, up and down the island.
People saw those photos and it changed them.
Something kicked up for them.
For us too.
All our friends from the whole island
are coming. My folks will be there too.
We've been thinking about these bigger movements
and what to learn from them," Zach adds.

"Think about the Dakota pipeline protests.
The Standing Rock Sioux Tribe got together
and then people followed. They didn't wait
for anything or anyone. They did it themselves.
We have to do that. Follow their lead.
Come together.
Just like the Hawaiian people at the foot
of Mauna Kea," Isa says, looking at me.

"We show up, and we don't leave.
We gotta look to Fridays for Future,
to Puerto Rico, to Bangladesh,
to New Orleans, to the global climate strikes.
We gotta take action.
They're doing it. Standing up
for what they want," Mia adds.

And then I realize

What really matters.
The earth.
The planet.
Our place
alongside it.
How to protect
hold
care for it.
This moment.
Right now.
Everything
that can't wait.

We can't wait
any
longer.

"We are the ones we have been waiting for"

"I keep thinking about June Jordan, and that quote
that Gloria shared with us," Mia says.

I repeat it over again in my mind.

"That's us right here. Right now. I love that.
Been carrying that around with me.
Knowing we can be the ones
that make the change," Zach says.

"Are you sure it's enough?
Does it need to be bigger?
Do we need more support?" I ask,
unsure if this is the right thing.

"Look, this is just a first step.
No one is gonna use a bulldozer
on a bunch of locals. You know that.
Let's show up and see what happens.
At least make our stand.
At least let them know how we feel," Isa adds.

"Camp out. That's what we have to do.
Get all our gear and go right after the clambake.
It's symbolic. Until they give us what we want,"
Zach finishes.

I smile. "I love you all.
I love your brilliant, genius minds.
I am in. It's us.
We're the ones who have to make the change."

They all smile right back at me.
Ready to take charge.

Clambake for the Climate
Rise Up with Us
See the Future

So we talk
and prep.
Meet up
each day
before
and after
work.
We work
set up.
Make calls.
Flyer.
Spread
the word.
Share
the news.
Remind
our people.
Even Milo.
I text him
to say

this is where

we will be

join us

if you

care

you

are

family.

My mom and Yara

enlist us to help cook.
So we become sous chefs.
Bakers. Me, Isa, Mia, and Zach
in the kitchen and fine-tuning
recipes. Making more and more.
Setting up tables and chairs.
Streamers and balloon set-ups
in the ball field behind the wharf.
My dad and Mr. Diaz build a stage
in the corner of the lot. Platform
for statements and the band.
The island feels transformed.
Everyone on the list. All are
welcome. Set up the speaker
system. Get our speeches
in order. Tell the *Sandpaper*
to run our final ad. Join us
at the LBI Clambake for the
Climate. For us. To save
the marshlands. To save
the planet. To save our
home.

The night of the clambake

We all get ready again
at my place. Nothing fancy
but dress in what feels right.
Jeans and Clam Cove Reserve T-shirts.

I put Milo far away from me
in the way back of my mind.
We turn on the music and dance.
Dance for the freedom to share
what's on our hearts. Dance
for this night. Dance for ourselves
and these friendships that feed us.
Dance for the changing tides
and how the ocean has always
carried us. Dance our way
to the ball field and the festival
we all made happen.

Everyone shows up

All of our families.
Jack and Ada. The Diaz Family.
Mateo and Rio and Marisol.
All our folks. And neighbors.
The lifeguards and baristas
from behind the counter.
Everyone who works
at the wharf. Cashiers
and line cooks. Surfers
and families with babies.
Tourists with their cameras
and fancy flip-flops.
Kids lined up for balloons
and face painting. Crews
and crews of people
hugging and laughing
and eating and drinking.
Already this is a crowd
rising and full around us.

The ball field looks out
on the bay and the setting sun.
Balloons in the shape
of dolphins and whales
line the entrance.
Booths set up
in each corner.
Sound system blasting.
People already on the dance floor.
Energy in the air.
This night is for everyone.

"This is what we planned for,"
Isa says, hugging me close.

We get to work at our different stations.
I sit in the front, welcoming
everyone. Tell them all about
the marshlands. What we are here
to protect. Tell them about growing
up on the island. How the hurricane
threatened everything about our life
and home. And especially how we're fighting back.

Zach is playing music—each song
building. Mia is helping Isa scoop
ice cream. Kids are running wild
from booth to booth. The coffee
and beer are flowing. People gathered
in all corners. Talking. Dancing.
Loving each other and this place.

We are about to close the front
and get the speeches started.
I look around one last time.
Hoping Milo will be here.
But he is nowhere in sight.
So I head in—without him.

Isa stands up first

She has been writing
and protesting
her whole life.
This is what she says:

"We protest with our bodies.
Protest with our whole selves.
Every vocal chord.
Alive and present.
We protest
with our hearts and lungs.
Our hands to the sky.
Hold on to the past,
while we fight for the future.
Call us brave and unmoved.
Call us fighters and full
of wisdom.
Don't call us kids,
or say we don't know
anything.
Don't make fun
of our voices
and how loud
and persistent they are.
We protest with our friends
and neighbors.
All the people who see us
and this land
as sacred.
As special
and ours to protect

and hold.
As full of life and honor.
Honor us.
Honor this.
By saving it."

I am up next

I am sharing a personal memory of the hurricane.
Of our family.

"Growing up on an island
can make you dream about sinking.
Living through a hurricane
can make you scared of everything.
Waking up to water below your bed.
Rushing through the doors
and windows of the only home you've ever known.
Your father's voice yelling for you to move, move.
And your mother wailing
as she collects old photographs and memories.
You can't hold
what you can't carry.
And we couldn't carry anything that day.
Everything pouring through our fingers.
Our arms heavy with loss.
I am here today to ask you all
to build with us.
Build the hope and memory
of this island.
Don't build condominiums
and massive homes
that will only sink us
again.
Join us to help
sustain. To help
us not just survive
but
thrive."

The clambake is a hit

We know this since it takes an extra
two hours to clean up. Good times
had by everyone and money raised
and food devoured and information
shared over and over.

Most of the adults clear out
and we are left gathering the trash
and clearing the ball field. Find
ourselves sitting out on the dock
after everything has been cleared up.

"Uh—where the hell was Milo tonight?"
Zach asks, sitting beside me, both of us
looking out on the water.

"Yeah. Everyone else was here. Like,
everyone else. Except for him. What's up?"
Isa wants to know.

"I didn't get to tell you all. But last week
I found out that his family is
behind the construction project,
the one for the marshlands.
They are the infamous Hope/Hart Construction team.
It's his dad, his stepmom. Essentially, it's him."

"Wait, what? The ones breaking ground
tomorrow?" Mia asks, standing up.
"Are you serious? Why didn't he tell us?"

"No clue. Actually, I don't know. I think
he didn't . . . doesn't think it's that big a deal.
And neither does my dad, since his team
got the bid to work on it.
So my kinda ex-boyfriend and my family
are behind the development
that we've been trying to stop.
But I guess none of that matters anymore.
I can't go to the sit-in," I say. Feeling defeated.
"I feel like a fake, a fraud."

"What? No, you're coming tonight"

Isa says. "So what if the people around you don't see it.
We do. You do. We're going. We're all going.
Eliza—basically the whole town is going.
We're meeting at one a.m.
My family gave me their blessing.
They know how hard we've been working.
You have to be there. This bond . . ."

"Unbreakable," we both say.
And I know she's right.
We ride home together.
Our bikes close
under the moonlight.
Stay near enough
to call out directions.

"Eliza . . . you did everything
you said you'd do this summer,"
Isa says, parked outside my house.

"Then why do I feel so bad?"

"That's on him. Not you.
He knew where we were tonight.
Knew how much this means
to all of us. That's on him.
And you know this place is our everything.
You know what the fight is."

I know she's right. I look up
at the sky. At our house,

rough around the edges.
All cobbled together.
I see the water.
See my brother
appearing
then disappearing.
See the mold
and how everything
felt ruined with water.
Felt ruined with the tides.

"See you at Clam Cove Reserve"

I say. Knowing there is no way
I could miss this, could miss
our moment. Can't stomach
bulldozers barreling through
to destroy the salt marsh,
the eggs of the terrapins
just nesting, just trying
to protect their way of life.
One of the most dynamic
and productive environments
on Earth can't be stopped
by greed and excess. By the desire
for more. With no regard
for such abundance.

"I won't miss it. One a.m. I'll be there.
Jack and Ada will too."

"I know. I love you," Isa says,
gives me a quick kiss on the cheek
and rides off.

When an emergency happens

Who do you call?
Who is there for you?
That is what I've been carrying with me.
The fear that it's not just one of us—it's all of us.
That this action could be dangerous.
That we could get in more trouble
than it's worth. Grounded. Arrested.
Not just me, but everyone around me too.
Knowing that Ada and Jack are packing supplies.
Food and water for everyone.
Loading their backpacks for the night and next day.
How long will we need to be there?
Will this action even matter?
Will they push against us, push us aside, push us out
of existence and pretend this island does not belong to us?
They would be right. It doesn't.
But we know deep down
it doesn't belong to more buildings
and more million-dollar homes
that weigh heavy on the land and our hearts.

We sneak out past midnight

Our folks fast asleep.
They know about the sit-in,
know about the protest.
My father started to stop us
and then realized
how much it means
and how invested we are.
He knows this is our fight.
We open the window out to the roof.
Go slow, I mouth at Jack and Ada.
They nod.
The night is cool on my skin—
knowing that summer is coming to a close.
Don't want to forget.
Don't want to get lost in these last hours,
in this moment.
I am both proud of us
and so scared that I'm shaking.
I go first, steady myself on the roof
and hold out my arm for Ada and then Jack,
and then all three of us are standing
there on the steady slope—surrounded
by a Jersey sky full of stars
and the biggest moon I've ever seen.

"So this is where you go every night?"
Ada asks, looking up at me.

"Yeah. Helps me clear my head.
Helped me figure this out.
Helped me not to be so scared."

Jack reaches for my hand,
and then so does Ada.
And I want to cry or sit to hold them there,
like we did the night of the hurricane,
like we've done so many nights since;
when one of us wakes up thinking we're sinking,
scared we're about to drown.

Moonlight

Once we hit the rocks in our front yard,
I see Milo standing beneath the streetlight,
his face glowing in the night.
He is carrying a surfboard,
not the fancy one he showed up with
two months ago, but the beat-up, classic board.
The one that takes effort to carry
while riding your bike.
He is standing, watching us.
I tell Ada and Jack to ride ahead
and we will meet them there.
And then it's just Milo and me.

"What are you doing here?" I ask

"I'm coming with you. To the protest,"
he says. "Zach told me everything.
I've been—I was trying to give you space.
Trying to figure out how I felt
about everything. About my dad.
About my stepmom, who is the one
that's been pushing this the most.
I needed to see what I was up against.
And I can't believe I missed the clambake.
I don't want to miss anything else,
and I miss you too much. I don't
want to miss you anymore.
And I spent the night reaching out
to all the news outlets. Let 'em know
that the developer's son was protesting
and would be there in the morning."

'What? You called the local stations?"

"Yeah. I figured they'd show up for that.
And thought I could at least do something
to help. Since I checked out on everything.
Since I checked out on you."

"Does your dad know?"

"He has no clue about what I did.
And he definitely doesn't know
about the protest
or that I'm gonna be there.
I'm here for you.

and the island.
I'm here for me too."

I can't help myself. I run to him.
Realizing I needed him to say that.
And need him here in this moment.

"Let's go then," I say, pulling his arm
and moving to the shed to get my bike.

"Wait. I need one more thing," he says,
and pulls me this time. Gentle and easy
toward him. His mouth on mine.
The moon in the sky
and everything in place.

We show up at one a.m.

and it's true.
Everyone we know
has shown up too.
All the lifeguards
propped up
by their boards.
And the fishing boats,
pulled in by the bayside
so they're sitting
edged into the marsh.
People are everywhere.
In tents
sitting on bicycles
and carrying boogie boards
and surfboards.
Spread out from Rosemma
to Beck Avenue—people
everywhere inside
the tall grasses.
Their faces
stretching to the sky.
All of our stories
unfolding here.
We gather
in pockets
and groups.

Knowing
when dawn
arrives
we will
not
be
moved.

My Heart

"Wanna take a walk?" Milo asks.
Still far away from morning.
Everyone laid out in packs.
No one is sleeping,
but everyone is calm and chill.

"Yeah. Let's walk to the beach,"
I say, and reach out for his hand.
It feels warm and perfect
inside mine.

We cross the empty street
from the marsh to the ocean.
I can hear the sound
of the waves.
Crashing up
and over again.
We walk the pathway
and down over the dunes.
The moon is high
in the sky.
Lighting up
everything.
I study Milo,
his shoulders
and jawline.
His hair piled
on top of his head.

"This is new," I say.
"This feeling. You.

Is all new to me.
I never expected this."

And then his hands
are holding my face
and he is leaning down
toward me.
Kissing me.
And my hands
find his stomach
and I can feel him
just start to shiver.

"It's new for me too,"
he says, into my ear.
He steps back. "I got something for you."

"For me?" I ask. Can hear the ocean
rushing in my head.

"This shirt," he says, unzipping his jacket.
It says: *I* ♥ *the Wave Whisperer.*
"And I always have," he whispers.

"What!? Are you serious?
You got that shirt made?
By a professional?"

"Oh no. Is it . . . it's cheesy.
This was too much. I know.
So weird."

We both start to laugh.

"But also kind of cool
and badass, right?"
he asks, slowing
turning around,
showing off.

"No, no. It's good.
It's perfect and exactly
what I needed to see.
I love it. I love it.
I love you," I say
in return.

"Come on then," he says

peeling off his shirt
and jeans and running off
to the water.

"What? Where are you . . . ?
What are we doing?"

"Going swimming," he says,
keeping his boxers on.
I run after him.
Taking off my jeans
and T-shirt too.
Keeping my bra
and underwear on.
It's just like a bathing suit
I say in my head.
My heart
as loud
as the ocean now.
Competing.
But he's running ahead,
not even looking behind.
Racing to the waves
all the way to his knees
and then waist
and I am running
full speed
behind him
to the salt
and the crashing
crashing

of the water.
The foam
up and over me
and we are out
to our shoulders
and I am floating
not scared
of sinking
anymore
not afraid
of the sea
or what damage
it could do.
It's already
done it all.

Dive underneath

and so does Milo
and all of a sudden
our arms
are shimmering
and shining
beneath.
Swirls of purple
and pink. Neon
below.

"What is this?"
Milo asks,
swimming up
and away
then back to me.

"Plankton," I call out
and watch it glow
below us.
Bioluminescence,
algae blooming
around us
sparkling
with each
break
of each
wave.

"You're glowing,"
he calls out,
swims right over

to me,
holds my waist
in the palms
of his hands
and we dunk clear
under a wave
and kiss
and the salt
and shimmer
surrounding us
makes us
luminescent
too.

We fall asleep on the beach

and wake up panicked.

"Come on. Let's go,"
I call, nudge Milo awake.

His arms are draped around me.
The two of us entwined.

I can't help but want this feeling
forever.

Back at the marshlands

we wait.
Trust my gut
and hold on.
No one has slept.
Just counted
the hours.
The news van
arrives first.
Asks for quotes
and interviews.
We talk
protest
and community.
Talk hurricanes
and the future.
What is needed
for protection
for safety
for health
for healing.
We talk climate
and environment
talk justice
and holding out
and hope.
Tell our stories
and why we're here
and what we're planning
to protect.

When the trucks arrive

Milo is standing front and center.
Our plan. The whole crowd on our feet.
They are planning a ribbon cutting,
but we are yelling.
Top of our lungs now. Shouting
for protection now. One Earth.
This planet is the one we are
protecting. Loving. Holding on to.

My mom and dad arrive.
My dad looks at me. I see him take us
and all of it in. He doesn't smile,
but I can see him holding off
running to me. He holds his hand
to the sky. Waves toward all of us.

The construction team is here
and Milo's dad shows up too.
His Escalade shiny and massive
on the street outside the marsh.
He walks out in shock. Olive
at his side. He sees Milo
and shakes his head. Sees us.
Sees the crowd gathered.
Sees the signs that say:

NO HOPE FOR THE HOPE/HART PROJECT

PROTECT THE MARSHLAND—AT ALL COSTS!

STAND UP FOR THE EARTH
STAND UP FOR OUR PLANET

On and on. We are a crew. A team.
This bond. Unbreakable.
Unstoppable.

The camera crew is fast—on Mr. Harris.
On Milo. On the crowd
cheering and yelling.

Mr. Harris pulls Milo to the side.
I hold my breath, while the crowd
stays loud. Stays fighting. Stays alert
and fierce beside me. Even though it's only
us, mostly teenagers, it feels like enough.

Feels like we could stop this

Like we could end it right here. Right now.

Milo stands forward in front of the camera
and says, "This project was a mistake
by my family. By my father. By me.
I see that now. And we are not moving."

The crowd starts to yell again.

"We are not leaving today," I say,
standing beside Milo now.
"Or tomorrow. Not until you all listen
to what the people of this island
actually want. Rather than telling us
what you think is best.
Trust us. This is our home
and we know the best ways
to protect it."

I stand back, flush with my own emotion
at finally getting the chance to say
how I really feel.

Mr. Harris is yelling at the crew. The noise
around us rising up, up. Olive is crying,
weeping beside him. In shock, she is shaking
her head at me and at Milo.
She doesn't even know us at all.

Finally, Mr. Harris makes an announcement.
Takes the megaphone and says this:

"I regret to say that we will not be breaking ground
on the Hope/Hart project today.
I apologize for the confusion."

I look over and Olive is wiping tears from her eyes.

"This is not the end—of course. And I am ashamed
that my son is a part of this mess. But we cannot
move forward today with so many of the locals here
who don't understand what we are trying to do,
and that we are here on this island to make it better.
And I hope this will be the start
of a conversation."

And as soon as he says it, the whole crowd cheers.
A loud eruption over the marshlands.
I know this is not over. Know this
could just be the beginning, but now
I know we shifted the day.
The movement
this moment.

Tomorrow,
the marshlands
will still be standing.

By afternoon

we make it
to the waves.
Shoreline
behind us.
All surfing
and catching.
See things
clearly now.
Wave
after wave
tries to take
us down.
But we see
the sand
settle.
My mind
begins to
go empty.
No fear.
No loss.
No destruction.
Just calm.
Just rest.
Just riding
until we reach
the sky.

Epilogue | After the storm

The sea is still here.
Where it has always been.
And our house. Rugged
and rough around the edges.
And the Diaz family.
Seven of us. Still riding
into the deep end
of every summer.
And Milo's house too.
Construction on his home
finished. Finalized.
Us moving
closer to neighbors
closer to in love
and staying that way.
The marshlands too.
A year later
still standing
still protected
still safe.
Long Beach Township
listening
and paying attention
and keeping the conversation
open and on us.
The township
moves to close
on twenty-four acres
of coastal marshlands
with the Ocean County
Natural Land Trust.

Clam Cove Reserve
belongs to the island
forever.

Forever Riding the Waves

"You know I'm almost as good as you now,"
Milo says, standing up while riding his bike.

Everyone starts to laugh at this. We are riding.
This crew—down the boulevard.
Family and friends and shouting
and laughing over the waves.

We ride.

"Keep dreaming," I call back,
lift my head and tilt it to the sky.

"Okay, I'll never be as good as you.
That's true," Milo says, pulling up
closer to me now.

"Just accept it.
I'm the only true
Wave Whisperer,"
I call back,
take the front

and lead us all

home.

ACKNOWLEDGMENTS

It is with such love that I call the names of all the friends & artists who have guided & shaped me—who have traveled this road with me. Thankful always for: Grisel Y. Acosta, Juan Acosta, E.J. Antonio, Stephanie Dionne Acosta, Lisa Ascalon, Jennifer Baker, Melanie Ballard Sewell, Julia Berick, Dan Bernitt, Berry, Leslie Hibbs Blincoe, Tokumbo Bodunde, Marc Boone, Cheryl Boyce-Taylor, Lori Brown-Niang, Susan Buttenwieser, Moriah Carlson, Kate Carothers Smith, Becca Christensen, Cheryl Clarke, Megan Clark Garriga, Olivia Cole, Angie Cruz, Brandi Cusick Rimpsey, LeConté Dill, Mitchell L. H. Douglas, Jason Duchin, Dana Edell, Kelly Norman Ellis, John Ellrodt, Kathy Engel, Maria Fico, Rajeeyah Finnie-Myers, D.A. Flores, Kevin Flores, Marsha Flores, Lisa Forsee Roby, Asha French, Tanya Gallo, Aracelis Girmay, Nanya-Akuki Goodrich, Catrina Ganey, Rachel Eliza Griffiths, Andrée Greene, Lisa Green, Ysabel Y. Gonzalez, Jake Hagan, Jen Hagan, Lisa Hagan, Michael Hagan, Karen Harryman, Lindsey Homra, JP Howard, Melissa Johnson, Amanda Johnston, Parneshia Jones, Carey Kasten, Caroline Kennedy, Michele Kotler, Mino Lora, Tim Lord, Rob Linné, Veronica Liu, Will Maloney, Alison McDonald, Caits Meissner, Stacy Mohammed, Yesenia Montilla, Andrea Murphy, Christina Olivares, Willie Perdomo, Andy Powell, Sarina Prabasi, Danni Quintos, Emily Raboteau, David Reilly, Carla Repice, Kate Dworkoski Scudese, Pete Scudese, Vincent Toro, Natalia Torres, Alondra Uribe, Jessica Wahlstrom, Crystal Wilkinson, Jenisha Watts, Renée Watson, Alecia Whitaker & Marina Hope Wilson.

Special & forever love to the original LBI crew: Britt Kulsveen, Kelly Wheatley & Megan Clark Garriga. Those summers will stay with me always.

To the Sunglass Menagerie crew & all the memories: Brett Russo, Alexis Julia, Kerry McMahon Dobis & Stephanie Anna—you will always make me think of salt water, sand & loving the ocean.

To my early & brilliant readers: Andy Powell, Renée Watson & Kelly Wheatley—thank you for elevating the story & asking all the best questions. So much love.

Thank you to Dani Pendergast for the most beautiful cover. Thank you for framing Eliza and the Jersey shore in such a stunning way.

Sarah Shumway Liu—what an immense joy to work with you. Your deep care & attention to this story & the way each poem arrived on the page was stunning & needed. Thank you always.

Thank you to the stellar team at Bloomsbury: Erica Barmash, Alexa Higbee, Beth Eller, Jasmine Miranda & Lily Yengle—for all the work you do to get our books ushered into the world.

Rosemary Stimola—you are such a superstar agent & I feel so lucky to be working with you & the beautiful team at Stimola Literary Studio—thank you.

For the collectives that helped to raise me as a writer & educator & activist: the Affrilachian Poets, Alice Hoffman Young Writers Retreat at Adelphi University, Café Buunni, Conjwoman, the DreamYard Project, Dodge Poetry Festival, Elma's Heart Circle, girlstory, Global Writes, International Poetry Exchange Program, Kentucky Governor's School for the Arts, New York Foundation for the Arts, Northern Manhattan Arts Alliance, Northwestern University Press, People's Theatre Project, Sawyer House, and VONA

Kamilah Aisha Moon: you live in my memory & heart always.

For my parents: Gianina & Patrick Hagan for bringing me to Long Beach Island, New Jersey. For your love of island living & protecting what you love most.

For David Flores. You are my forever. What luck to love this much. Here is to always creating, living & loving. Together.

Always for my daughters—Araceli & Miriam. You two are my whole world. Keep reaching, keep raising your voices, keep rising up. Keep writing yourselves into existence. Exist—always.

My love for the ocean and the community of Long Beach Island, New
Jersey, runs deep. My mother grew up every summer in Harvey Cedars
and was a lifeguard on the bay beach, and so I too grew up spending
every summer down the shore. Eventually my family had a home in
Holgate, New Jersey. We saw the devastation brought on by Hurricane
Sandy firsthand and were there as the community began to rebuild.
Barrier islands are a high-risk environment. They face rising sea levels,
storm surges, disappearing dunes, erosion, vulnerability of coastal
infrastructure, and increased tropical storms that are happening with
intense and devastating frequency. Our human impact on the coastal
ecosystems and communities is dire. It is our job to continue to learn
how to navigate our relationship to a changing planet. I wrote this
story to honor and celebrate the ocean and the people who call it
home. I wrote this story as a bridge to connect one small island to
islands all around the world, knowing this issue is both local and
global. I also wrote this as a way to address my own constant anxiety
and fear of climate change. I needed to hold both parts of the story.
The more I read about and studied the effects of global warming, the
more I unearthed young people fighting back and creating real and
sustained change in the world.

    In *Don't Call Me a Hurricane*, you met fictionalized characters
who are working together to make real and impactful changes in their
community. Below is information about some real-life artists, activists,
and writers who are changing the landscape through dialogue and
clear actions. I am so moved and inspired by the youth climate
activists who are rising up and fighting for environmental justice.
These young people are using their voices, their connections to the
natural world, and their skills at organizing and community building
to make a real and lasting difference. As an artist, activist, educator,
and mother, I am activated by this multigenerational collective

building—how we show up and come together as a community. These young activists are my guide, and I hope you will follow the threads here and find out what organizations, activists, and books speak to you. I look so forward to hearing your voices and rising up alongside of you.

ORGANIZATIONS TO LEARN MORE ABOUT

Center for Native American Youth: https://www.cnay.org/

Climate Justice Alliance: Communities United for a Just Transition: https://climatejusticealliance.org/

Climate Museum: Culture for Action: https://climatemuseum.org/

Communities for a Better Environment: Building Community Power to Achieve Environmental Justice, Clean Energy and Healthy Communities: https://www.cbecal.org/

Earth Guardians: https://www.earthguardians.org/

Earth Uprising: https://earthuprising.org/

Environmental Justice Foundation: https://ejfoundation.org/

Fridays for Future: https://fridaysforfuture.org/

Future Coalition: https://futurecoalition.org/

Honor the Earth: https://www.honorearth.org/

Indigenous Environmental Network: https://www.ienearth.org/

International Indigenous Youth Council: https://indigenousyouth.org/

Intersectional Environmentalist: https://www.intersectionalenvironmentalist.com/

Long Beach Island Foundation of Arts + Sciences: https://lbifoundation.org/

Re-Earth Initiative: https://reearthin.org/

Sunrise Movement: https://www.sunrisemovement.org/

SustainUS: U.S. Youth for Justice and Sustainability: https://sustainus.org/

350.org: https://350.org/

Uplift: https://upliftclimate.org/

UPROSE: https://www.uprose.org/climate-justice

We Act for Environmental Justice: https://www.weact.org/

The Youth Climate Strike: https://strikewithus.org/

MORE BOOKS TO READ

*The No-Nonsense Guide to Climate Change: The Science, the Solutions,
the Way Forward* by Danny Chivers

The Marrow Thieves by Cherie Dimaline

This Is Not a Drill: An Extinction Rebellion Handbook by Extinction Rebellion

*As Long as Grass Grows: The Indigenous Fight for Environmental Justice,
from Colonization to Standing Rock* by Dina Gilio-Whitaker

The Future Earth: A Radical Vision for What's Possible in the Age of Warming
by Eric Holthaus

*The Story of More: How We Got to Climate Change and
Where to Go from Here* by Hope Jahren

*Braiding Sweetgrass: Indigenous Wisdom, Scientific Knowledge, and the Teachings
of Plants* by Robin Wall Kimmerer

*How to Change Everything: The Young Human's Guide to Protecting the Planet
and Each Other* by Naomi Klein with Rebecca Stefoff

*We Rise: The Earth Guardians Guide to Building a Movement that Restores
the Planet* by Xiuhtezcatl Martinez

Frontlines: Stories of Global Environmental Justice by Nick Meynen

War Girls by Tochi Onyebuchi

One Earth: People of Color Protecting Our Planet by Anuradha Rao

Paradise on Fire by Jewell Parker Rhodes

Taking on the Plastics Crisis by Hannah Testa

No One Is Too Small to Make a Difference by Greta Thunberg

WRITERS AND YOUTH ACTIVISTS TO LEARN MORE ABOUT

Vic J. Barrett
Xiye Bastida
Octavia E. Butler
Katie Eder
Mary Annaïse Heglar
Isaias Hernandez
Isra Hirsi
Kathy Jetñil-Kijiner
June Jordan
Jamie Margolin
Xiuhtezcatl Martinez
Nadia Nazar
Varshini Prakash
Emily Raboteau
Hannah Testa
Leah Thomas
Greta Thunberg
Alexandria Villaseñor
David Wallace-Wells
Elizabeth Yeampierre